In memory of Jeff Klitzner.

For Memphis, for being exactly what it is.

Memphis Dirty:
Tales From The Dirty South

Table of Contents

Introducing Memphis

Memphis, Tennessee is a dirty place. I'm not talking so much about trash being all over the streets, because I've seen much worse. No, I'm talking about the spirit of the city: it's a place of low expectations and dirty people, a place that doesn't expect too much of itself. It's not like the capital city, Nashville, which is full of up-and-comers and really out to make something fancy of itself. See, Memphis doesn't try too hard to be something it's not; it's got problems, and it's okay with that. That's one reason I feel more comfortable there, because it's a lot like me: we're comfortable with ourselves, even though we're jacked up.

Besides being one of the largest cities in the United States, Memphis routinely competes for the most violent city in the country. Truthfully, it often ranks among the most violent places in the world. I did the math, and while I was in Baghdad, Iraq, during the Surge, I was seven times more likely to die a violent death at home than I was in a warzone, where there was an internationally-funded and organized terrorist army actually out to get me. Here, I would have just been killed at random by some jack-ass, likely in one of our world-class car-jackings.

Memphis is the kind of place pizza delivery guys get killed for the $4 they had on them by hood rats, riding their bicycle around at night with a shotgun in their lap. We can't have nice things in Memphis, because the young bucks who think they're going to kill somebody and become the next Tu-Pac are a dime a dozen.

I've heard it said that the Indians who lived in the area didn't settle down in Memphis, instead going down a bit to modern Southaven, Mississippi. Why? Because Memphis was haunted, a place where the souls of the grouchy dead got together. If you've ever been in Memphis, you'll find it hard to argue with that.

Memphis is the true birthplace of the blues and rock and roll (screw you, Cleveland) and gave American culture a lot of our most precious music and greatest tragedies. It has the best bar-b-que in the world, but we've had two kings here and killed them both.

Memphis started out as a den of thieves, harlots, and drug-heads out to win a quick buck. Not much has really changed. But since Memphis and its people know how jacked up they are, it's alright to celebrate it for what it is: one of the most inspiring places in the world. I don't mean inspiring like: "skyscrapers that reach unto the very edge of Heaven", "alive with fresh artistry straight from the cutting edges, or "a nice place to raise your children". I mean inspiring like how you can look at an ugly dog and laugh, or can't help but watch a car crash. You might find you even come to love the place.

In tribute to that city of legend, some proud and some not-so-proud Memphians and I have put together this collection of short stories we hope helps bring Memphis to your thoughts again and again. Welcome to Memphis.

Stephen Clements
Editor

The Teahouse of Vile Revolution
By Stephen Clements

"WE WILL CONQUER THEM WITH OUR VICES!" read the plaque over the door to the Teahouse of Vile Revolution, before Operation Phase-10 would come crashing down all around them. But, as is said, all in its own good time, whether it's a good time or not.

Act 1: The Desolation

Reo was his name. Smoking a Lucky Strike cigarette on the street corner, he waited. He waited for the others to show. It was a hot summer's night, the wet brick and concrete glistening in the yellow streetlight.

There was a splashing of water in the gutter, and a mean old man with yellow, mulatto skin came humping along with his cane in his hand, more a weapon than a support. Blind Apricot Harding meant business tonight. "What's the score, young slacka'?" he said to Reo.

"We's waitin' on da rest of dem, ol' man. Yuh bring yo' birfday presunts?"

"Bitch, you think I leave home without it?!" ol' Apricot groaned, violently shaking his cane at the young gun. "I'll show you young punks how to settle a score!"

"POP, BITCHES!" sounded out of the darkness, as a small, wiry young man jumped out of the shadows with a showman's flourish.

Reo didn't jump at the dip-stick bounding out of the alleyway across the street. Reo was too cool for that.

Ol' Apricot was too mean to flinch. "4-way, you botha' puttin' on de-odorant today? 'Cuz I don't want to be smellin' yo' cheap ass all night," barked Apricot.

"4-way" had a real first name (Derrell), but what other men would try to bury as a shameful incident that they never wanted to recall, he took as a place of pride in his life's accomplishment.

"You want some gum, ol' man? I can smell yo' aufritis breaf from here," 4-way thought he wittily retorted.

"Whuz up, guys?" asked Jerome, a fat, young man in a sweater and jacket that always looked too small on his tall frame, as he lumbered onto the scene.

That's everybody, Reo calculated. That'll be enough.

"So we gonna whip some ass or stare at each other all night? We got some honor to A-VENGE!" boasted ol' Harding.

"Listen, ol' man, I don't know why we're makin' a big deal out of it. Every beauty's got ta go out wiff an idiot," said 4-way.

"Is that how you keep getting dates, stank ass?" asked Apricot.

Plaid sleeves and bare limbs flew in the air, as the two went at each other. The smaller men were quickly separated by big man Jerome.

"Can we just save it for the real enemy, guys? Just this once?" pled the big man with a kind face.

While 4-way continued squaring off by himself, old Harding acquiesced.

The wizened man spoke, saying, "Man, I just get all worked up wit' a quickness, when one of my girls gets hurt like that."

"Let's go," Reo said calmly. "Too much talkin', time to get stompin'." He dropped his cigarette, leaving it hissing on the ground.

The posse followed him into the tearoom, an abandoned diner built when Memphis knew a better, less violent age. They grabbed things they'd need from boxes, pantries, and hiding spots: handcuffs, wire, a bag of fertilizer, a can of gasoline, and a half-drunk bottle of Hennessy thrown in for the road. They came here for a noble purpose, even if they were about to get dirty. They had a disgraced angel to avenge.

Act 2: The Descent

The ratty, day-glow door flew off its rusty hinges with a bang, blowing up a cloud of dirt and cigarette butts in its wake. At the far end of a dilapidated, shotgun shack just off South 3rd Street, Leon sat enthroned, his white suit and straight, black hair unimpressed by the dramatic intrusion. Three bloods moved protectively from behind his chair, trying to appear united while concealing their fear. They had expected retaliation for what their boss had done to that poor woman, and now it had come.

"That's right, mutha fuckas! We up in this shit like dat!" pronounced 4-way as he bounded to the front of the room. Twirling a Little League Slugger, he made room for Reo, Harding, and Jerome to march in for the slaughter.

Lowering his smoldering cigar from his lips with a grace earned from abandoning church, Leon asked, "What's this about, Reo?"

"It's about HONOR, you punk!" bellowed the cane-shaking Apricot, trembling with fury. Reo nodded once, because that's all that needed to be said.

It was on.

"It ain't got to go down like this, Reo. Let the past lay," said Leon, accompanied by the sound of his fist rocking a scrawny jaw and the 4-way attached to it hitting the floor.

"Wut you did ain't cool, Leon. You busted MY MOMZ, TRICK!" Reo shouted, finally losing his cool and clenching his eyes in rage.

8

One of Leon's boys charged Reo, but the battle-ready Harding clocked him with a hard right and a string of expletives.

Jerome jumped between two thugs and 4-way's crying body, shovel in hand. Reo went at Leon, swinging his bike chain like a man possessed. Leon stood placidly, parrying and deflecting Reo's metallic assault with the mastery of his chrome dice-capped pimp stick.

"PANG" declared a solid shot against one of the thugs' skulls by Jerome in this epic struggle. Apricot wasn't so lucky, as he got hit by another thug, and then he hit the floor, his cane scuttling away from him across the scuffed-up floor.

"Boy-toy, toss me the Hennessy!" he implored 4-way. "And quit cryin', you little skillet! Get in da fight: PUT JO' WEIGHT ON IT!"

4-way lay there crying, as Jerome got tackled into the wall beside him. The old man helpless, Reo swept the almost empty bottle to the seasoned citizen, all the while still whipping his bike-chain like mad at the villain who started all this.

Leon's hair was unperturbed by this pathetic offensive.

Licking his stubbly lips as he groped the bottle, old Harding swigged down the contents before throwing it in a beautiful overhand arc straight into the back of the dude who was kidney-punching Jerome senseless. The thug went down, much to the wheezing fat boy's salvation.

"For Reo's momma," Jerome breathed weakly, as he brought the shovel down again. Rushing unsteadily to help the chain-wielding Reo, a swift planting of Leon's chrome-topped cane in his face sent Jerome to his back, out cold.

Reo seized the moment of distraction and slapped Leon like a bitch on a toilet. That was the last thing he and his friends would remember that night.

9

Act 3: Denouement

Reo came to, his left eye swollen shut and the taste of cigarette smoke and metal in his mouth. Squatting beside him, Leon's white suite was pristine. His hair was slightly mussed.

"Look, man, I just spoke the truth. We didn't have to do it like this," said Leon in a kind voice.

"REVENGE!" shrieked old Apricot, still stuck on his seized back.

"Chill out, old man," Leon spat over his shoulder, without malice in his voice

"IT WAS HIS MOMZ, YO!" squealed 4-way, now tied to a folding chair.

Leon's caramel face grimaced, as he raised the back hand of his hand to the young moron. Just the threat was enough to shut him up.

Jerome slouched against the poster-riddled wall. He was still breathing, but out cold.

Raising his elbows on the dirty fast food wrappers all over the floor, Reo protested, "You broke her, Leon. How's she supposed to go on now? You took everything away from her!"

"That old turkey was dry, man. That's just a fact. Weren't no gravy, neither," Leon spoke consolingly, but firmly. "I just said what everybody at the church potluck was thinking."

Reo looked thoughtful. "Well, you right. You still coming to dinner Sunday afta church?"

"Tell your mom I can't wait for more of her fried chicken," Leon offered, extending his right hand to help Reo off the filthy floor.

"Aight," said Reo, taking Leon's hand.

Peace had come at last to the ghetto.

Restraint
By Joseph Tate

"I don't know why we need all this," I told Mark, the male nurse on duty. "You guys know I'm easy-going. When was the last time anybody had to lay hands on me?"

Mark nodded, the crow's feet around his eyes crinkling in mild humor. "You know the drill, man. Here, every patient gets the same four-star treatment."

Mark was a good guy. Under different circumstances, we would have been fast friends. But not now. Now, regardless of when or where we met, I would always be one of his ex-patients from the Memphis VA Hospital Psychiatric Ward.

"Just do me one favor, man," I said to Mark. "Try to act like you don't enjoy it so much."

Mark's smile spread from his eyes to the rest of his face. "Yeah," he said, smirking, "putting your big ass in leather restraints is my idea of a dream come true."

It was Tuesday, and Tuesday was electro-convulsive therapy day. My psychiatrist, Dr. Samuel K. Brueller, entered "The Quiet Room" as Mark finished putting me in restraints. Dr. Brueller never seemed to be around unless there was a male orderly present, I was tied down, or both. I don't know what the deal with Dr. Brueller was, but I do know that he reminded me of one of those guys we'd get in Vietnam: the kind of fuckin' new guy who everybody just knew was going to get lots and lots of people killed…unless we got him killed first.

"Seems like our patient is ready for a little electric sunshine," Dr. Brueller said. His smile was so fake, so obviously put-on that I don't think that even he believed it. Dr. Brueller seemed to notice more of an improvement from every Tuesday's round of shock treatments than I did, but I guess my last name didn't have enough letters behind it to get a fair vote.

Mark inspected the restraints in silence. He kept busy fiddling with the restraints; I'm sure Dr. Brueller had given him orders not to leave us alone together. I liked Mark, so I didn't press the issue.

"Today is a bit of an anniversary for you, Mr. Johnson," Dr. Brueller said, drawing my attention back to him. He had this habit of looking just past you as he spoke, as if there was something just off your shoulder much more fascinating than you. "You are due for your twenty-fourth ECT. That's a facility record!" Dr. Brueller sniffed, his eyes darting around the room, as he edged just a bit closer to the door.

"I know that, Doc, just like you know my name is Otis, not Mr. Johnson."

Dr. Brueller ignored my calling him "Doc" (something I did as often as possible, knowing that he hated to be called that) and continued speaking as if I had not actually said anything. "We've only been doing ECT for three years, since 1978, in fact. Most patients' benefits are achieved within just a few sessions. Unfortunately, your symptoms have been extremely persistent."

I made it a point to speak to Dr. Brueller as little as possible, partly because I had nothing to say to the bastard, partly because he called flashbacks "persistent symptoms", but mostly because it made him uncomfortable. "So what, Doc?" I said. "About another dozen or so oughta finish what the Viet Cong couldn't? After all, what's a little shock therapy between friends?"

As I spoke, Dr. Brueller's left hand eased out of his perfectly pressed lab coat and touched the edge of the door. "I'll see you shortly, first thing, first thing." Tails of his lab coat flying, Dr. Brueller turned and fled the room.

The entire time that Dr. Brueller and I were talking, or rather Dr. Brueller was talking at me, Mark had been quietly loosening my restraints. He'd left me enough room on the stretcher to turn on my side. Mark knew how sick I got after the electro-convulsive therapy.

"Ready to ride?" he asked. Mark treated me like a kid brother, even though I was almost fifteen years older than him, and at 6' 4", I was almost ten inches taller and at least a solid hundred pounds heavier.

"Home, Mark," I said. And away we went.

Unlike the other nurses, Mark kept quiet as he rolled me down the winding halls of the Memphis Veterans Hospital to my weekly ECT appointment. After all, I was about to have my memories literally shocked out of my brain, so the last thing I wanted to do was chat, or be chatted at.

When we pulled up just outside the ECT room, Mark stopped the stretcher and came around to the side. "What do you want for afterwards?" he asked.

This was another reason I liked Mark so much: he didn't make me ask him. "Can you get Diana Ross to swing by my room?" I said, keeping my face straight.

"Same request as last week," Mark said, smiling.

"Guess not then," I said. "If you can't get Diana Ross, I guess a lunch tray will have to do."

Mark nodded. His thinning hair shook and glinted in the fluorescent light, which put off an acrid smell, like something being welded. "You got it, man," he said, as he pushed me into the ECT room.

ECT is rough. It's rough on me, and I did two tours in Vietnam. I was captured and tortured, and I had to crawl through twenty miles of jungle to escape. I'd never admit it, because Marines aren't supposed to be scared of anything, but I am afraid of that room. Really afraid. The IV isn't the problem:

shots and needles don't bother me. There's just something about ECT that gets to me.

I tried to tell Dr. Brueller that the room smells. I told him that every time I'm in that room, I can smell the jungle, which wouldn't be so bad, except that I smell jungle in Tennessee, and that's just retarded. But it's not just the jungle I smell. It's the craziest thing: the smell of overwhelming green, or nature growing unchecked, is so fuckin' strong. There is a hint of carbon, like rounds have recently been fired, and a whiff of something else. Something I know I know, but can't fully recall. Something dark and moist, like cold rain on a deep winter night, but darker and intentional. I know it's crazy, but I sure as shit can smell that rain every time I get ECT.

Just before the technician starts the shock treatments, I hear the first raindrops of what may be either a sprinkle or a monsoon, just before they hit the canopy. The thing is that in 'Nam, rain brought bad things, really bad things. Sometimes when I wake up from ECT, I feel the raindrops on my skin. I know it's not raining; I mean, my brain knows, but still, for just a few minutes, I'm back with my recon team, in the Annam Highlands, laying on my back, letting the rain wash the darkness from my soul. In those few minutes after I first come out of ECT, it's still 1968. At least for me it is.

"Count backward from 100," the technician said. I could already feel whatever he had given me hitting my system.

"99, 98, 97," I began. And then the ground fell away from the world.

The rain in Vietnam doesn't always fall. Sometimes, quite often in fact, it drives itself into the ground, as if in a hurry to get back to heaven. This was that kind of rain.

Sergeant Johnson and his fire team, being Corporals Evans and Mitchell, Private First Class Moehle, Private

14

Shallenberger and their guide, a Montagnard native named Trang, were deep in the Annam Highlands tracking the movements of a Viet Cong patrol said to have set up operations in the area. The fire team followed barely visible tracks for weeks through jungle so dense, so isolated that no non-Vietnamese eyes had probably ever seen it.

Sgt. Johnson held up his fist palm out, and his team stopped. They had been close, really close, to the Viet Cong platoon until two days ago when the rain came. Corporals Evans and Mitchell and Trang slid through the muck to Sgt. Johnson's position.

"Any sign of 'em?" Sgt. Johnson asked.

He liked Trang. Trang was one of those people who could look you right in the eye, smile, and spill your guts on the ground before you even knew you'd been cut. That was one of Sgt. Johnson's favorite personality traits for a soldier under his command to have.

"No, Huynh," Trang said. Trang insisted on calling each of the team members Vietnamese names. Sgt. Johnson was Huynh, or "older brother". "We fucked bad to-night," Trang continued. It wasn't Trang's mutilation of the English language that made him hard to listen to: it was his love of profanity.

"What the hell does that mean, Trang?" Corporal Mitchell asked through clenched teeth.

"You no worry, Die^'n," Trang said. "We bad fucked e-ry night."

"Seriously though," Corporal Mitchell added, "we can't just crawl around the entire jungle 'till we find 'em. Come on Sarg, let's make camp and wait out the rain."

Sgt. Johnson nodded. Not that any of them could see him do it, with no moonlight.

"Trang," Sgt. Johnson said, "Can you find us a room with a view?"

Trang's broad, brown face split with a wide smile. "Sure 'nuff, Huynh, I find. And I find nice spot for you all, and something special for Trang special friend Sang."

Trang and Mitchell, or "Sang", as Trang called him, hated each other. In different circumstances, one or both of the men would already be dead.

"My fuckin' name is Terry James Fuckin' Mitchell, Trang." Mitchell hated all things Vietnamese. He was one of those guys who came to Vietnam young, too young, and full of promise. Every day he spent here, he died a little inside.

"Alright people," Sgt. Johnson said. "Time to get the machine moving. Mitch, you take point; Evans, get the rear. And Evans," Sgt. Johnson paused, making sure he had Evans' full attention. "Don't get left behind this time, alright?"

They all liked Corporal Kevin Evans the way you like a kid brother that just can't keep up: try as hard as he can, Evans was always a step behind. Trang's Vietnamese name for Evans, "Farm", suited Evans' personality just right. Evans was better suited to tilling fields than mucking through a tour in 'Nam. But there was no one on the team who was a better shot.

In spite of not looking it, Evans was smart. He spoke fluent Vietnamese, and he knew that Trang's name for Mitchell meant a person who acted like he was upper class, which, in fact, Mitchell was, and that Trang meant it as an insult.

Evans smiled his "aw shucks" smile and slid back towards the two Privates.

"You alright, Mr. Johnson?" the technician asked.

"Sure…fine," was all I could squeeze through my tortured throat. "Is it over?" I asked the technician.

"No, sir. We had some difficulty keeping you under. I'm going to need you to relax a bit, Mr. Johnson. Can you do that for me?"

16

I looked at the wires hooked to my bare chest, the leather straps on my wrists and ankles, and the IV pumping God-knows-what into my veins. "Sure, buddy…relaxation in 5, 4, 3…"

"The problem with ambushes," Evans said, "is that you don't know they're comin'."

The team was taking heavy fire from both sides. After tracking the Viet Cong platoon for almost three weeks, they'd walked right into an ambush. Sgt. Johnson wasn't in a talkative mood, as he was busy trying to simultaneously fire left and right with his M60.

"Get your ass down and your muzzle up, Evans!" Mitchell shouted.

For a time, the only sounds the team made were with their weapons. Sgt. Johnson, with the M60, spoke loud and often. Mitchell, with an M16, spoke in deadly spurts. Trang, with the AK-47, sounded muted and foreign, but intense. Evans, with the sniper rifle, spoke infrequently, but every time he uttered a sound, a body dropped to the jungle floor. The two Privates "Johnson-ed" the tree line: instead of firing their weapons, they did nothing except throw grenades like baseballs of death, deep into the trees.

Sgt. Johnson knew that like all the previous fire fights that he'd been in, there would come a point where one of three things was going to happen: Charlie was going to get dead; his team was going to get dead; or someone was going to have to run like hell. Sgt. Johnson didn't think that tonight was the night for his team to count Viet Cong bodies.

"Fellas," Sgt. Johnson said, "time to get to gettin'!" Sgt. Johnson knew that the Viet Cong platoon was split on at least two sides, and he had to pick a clear path for the team. He had no way of knowing whether or not he was running into the teeth of the enemy. So they ran, Sgt. Johnson leading the way, firing his M60 from his hip John Wayne-style and running for all he was worth.

The rain kept the smell of weapons fire close to the ground. I lay there, feeling the rain drum on my skin, smelling fear and death, and hearing my blood pound in my ears. I was, for the first time in the eighteen months I'd been in 'Nam, scared. I tried to move, but I was tied down. When had I been captured?

"Just relax, take it easy," a voice said. I'd heard that some of the Viet Cong spoke perfect English. I kept my eyes closed tight. If I see him, if I see his face, he'll have to kill me to protect his cover.

"Where's my team?" I asked. I hadn't gone down by myself. Mitchell and Trang were right behind me, firing like hell, when I took off running, and I could hear the little booms from the Privates' grenades.

"Your team?" the interrogator asked.

I had either been captured by myself, or this Commie bastard was already beginning the psychological torture.

"Just relax here a minute. I'll be right back," the interrogator said.

I knew from my P.O.W. training that the best time to escape was immediately after capture. I crept my eyes open just enough to see him leave the room, probably to get more interrogators. Luckily, my restraints were loose enough so that I could turn on my side. I used the available space to thrash myself whip-like and snap the restraints.

Once I was free, restraints trailing, I sprang off the cot. I knew that the noise would bring trouble. For some reason, I was barefoot, with only a pair of thin pants on. I hid behind the door, scrunched down. The stench of death mingled with ozone and something else, something antiseptic. Blood still pounding in my ears, I crouched and waited, repeating my team's names over and over.

"Evans, Trang, Mitch…all gone, gone," I mumbled. I only had to wait a few minutes before the interrogator came back into the room. He walked right past me, saw the empty cot, and before he could turn around, I used one of the straps to snap his neck. It was a fast death, better than he deserved.

I felt a push from behind as another Viet Cong tried to tackle me. This guy was small, light. I reached back, grabbed what was left of his hair, and tossed him against the wall. He hit hard, bounced off the wall and slammed to the floor.

He started to rise to his knees.

"Don't speak you fuck!" I yelled. "You bastards killed 'em all, even Evans!"

The guy was scared, real scared. "No, Otis," he said, "it's me…"

Before he could finish, my hands were around his throat. "No Viet Cong lies! There's nothing you can say that can bring them back, is there?"

And then I snapped his neck. "That's for Trang, you fuck," I said, then spat on his dead body. I figured that I'd only have a short time before all Hell broke loose. I slipped into the hallway, padding quietly. I was going to have to get back to headquarters and let them know about this place. None of our recon had reported that the Viet Cong had anything as sophisticated as this!

I wandered the halls, lost for what seemed like hours. After a time, the smell of the jungle began to diminish. I no longer felt the rain on my skin, and I could hear again.

Tired, I slipped into a supply closet to rest. I slept for a time, fitfully. My dreams were of violent episodes from Vietnam, mostly; my dreams were of an ambush on a hillside deep in the Annam Highlands. Times I don't want to remember, but can't forget.

The River Hippies Like Me
By Jeff Klitzner

It happened one day, while I was exploring the banks of the Wolf River in a small town out east of Memphis. I wasn't paying too much attention to the world around me, aside from the Guns and Roses CD blasting from the rather large boom box I was carrying. It was 2005 or 2006, I think. I'm not really sure which, because the whole date/year-thing never really mattered much to me. On this walk, I was examining the darkest regions of my past over and over again in my mind.

I kept replaying things I had fucked up in my life, people I had hurt and who had hurt me. Maybe if I did that enough, I'd remember that things didn't really happen that way, that the world didn't actually have the scars I thought it had. Maybe things would be better, if life really didn't turn out like it did.

That's when I caught the stench that was familiar to me at one point in my life. Well, okay, for my entire life. As the stench of sweet, stanky weed hit my nostrils, I knew it was only fit and proper for me to find the source, introduce myself, and see if I could bogart some of that fellowship.

As I walked down past the used tires that had washed up on the riverbank, I couldn't help but think to myself, "Man, it's been a while since I've seen a hippie smoking a joint rolled with actual papers, and not those nasty, cheap cigar wraps." Now I could feel that I was getting close, and as I walked up to a clearing in the grass on the riverbank, I noticed two men and three women sitting around on what could only be described as a raft made of plywood and several inner-tubes tied together, with a large tent resting on top. They were floating just off the muddy bank, anchored by some make-shift device. Potheads all think they are the next coming of MacGuyver, because where there's a will, there's a way. Especially if getting high is at the end of the rainbow.

As I was walking up, my anticipation grew. When I hit the muddy bank, my stride changed up: like a natural instinct, I went from a casual stroll to dropping my knee almost to the ground followed by a twist of my hips to pull it back up. It was a way to stay unstuck in that much muck, and it went like gang-busters, even though I hadn't done that in years. My boots were almost gliding across the top of the mud, but I got cocky and tripped on the tires. I lost control of my boom box, and the CD skipped. I could see a few heads poking up and turning towards me, and I heard the voices mumbling.

I was now faced with a hard choice: I could get my tunes or my body to safety on the plywood refuge that was floating closer to me, but not both, as gravity was once again trying to push me down. (Let me explain that bit about gravity: see, a lot of people think gravity is pulling you down, but they're wrong. Gravity is pushing you down, like the Man trying to keep you down. Mother Nature is the first and greatest oppressor) I wasn't happy with the choices, so I did the first thing that popped into my head when confronted with danger: Stop, Drop, and Roll! With my roaring boom box flying through the air towards the raft, bumping that classic by Hall and Oates "Out of Touch" as it went, I leapt out of my roll and landed on the raft like a mackerel aboard a fishing vessel's deck. I flopped from my stomach to my back and caught my most prized possession, just as it grazed the top of the shallow water. It's called skills, don't hate.

At this point, I couldn't help but notice the three dirty, hairy people lying beneath me. I also saw an outstretched hand with a joint in it. It was pointed flame-out, as was custom amongst polite smokers offering to one another. Of course, I accepted and then gently rolled off the two ladies and one rather confused gentleman. We all sat up, and I took two puffs off that sweet, sweet weed. Being a good person, I then passed it to the left. After exhaling, I began to speak with my new-found friends, figuring I could at least introduce myself. You know, after jumping on them and smoking their weed.

"I apologize for my rude intrusion onto your vessel, but I have never been able to resist the sweet aroma that is now before me. I trust none of you were harmed in the demonstration of my Magic Ninja Powers? My given name is Jeff, but my friends call me Tennessee," I said, looking concerned.

They stared at me, glassy-eyed and expecting something else. I flashed my blunt, toothy grin, and the urge to laugh overcame us all. After a few more rounds of uncontrollable laughter, the man I landed on spoke.

"My name is Mark, and this is my soul-mate Jennifer. That's Harry, but he doesn't talk anymore: he gave that up a few months ago," he trailed off.

He was followed by the blonde I fell on, who said, "I'm Monica, and this is my sister Lilly. She is kind of shy. I think she likes you already."

Before I could say anything, Lilly pulled a flower out of her hair and offered it me; it was she who had offered me the joint upon my landing. I accepted the flower, and it happened to be my turn in the circle for another toke. Finding myself on this raft with the free-love types, I decided it would be rude for me to not ask about the vessel and their unique habitat.

Before I could speak, though, Mark asked me with great intensity, "How did you gain your Magic Ninja Powers?" I could tell the concept was causing bouts of deep thought in him.

I explained that I was one of the select few members of the only truly top-secret organization in the world, known as the Supreme Soviet. The questions began to follow, but I had to keep mum. I had already said too much: I knew the penalty for those who spoke too much about our role in modern society. Hell, I came up with the penalty, so it wasn't pleasant thinking about what I would have to do to myself if I said any more.

I quickly changed the subject. "Hey, silent dude, why did you give up speaking?"

He proceeded to make a bunch of random hand gestures, and I couldn't figure out what the hell he was doing.

"You look like a quadriplegic having a seizure," was the only sensible response.

He didn't look too pleased. Then his chick said, "He went mute, so he could better understand the value of a word."

Mark asked me, "Why do you place such value on your boom box? You shouldn't value your possessions so much."

I informed him, "The value isn't monetary, neither is it for status. Rather, I have a deep, emotional connection to that song, as it helps me control my emotions."

Lilly asked me, "Why would you want to control your emotions?"

I couldn't help but feel bad for her young heart. It was obvious she had never known the pain of a heart breaking, nor the satisfaction of knowing that life is nothing more than a series of random daggers to the heart. I began to explain that while life has many beautiful things in it, the one constant in my life has been tragedy. I could tell by the look in their eyes that I had thrown them a line, and they bit.

I looked up to see the setting sun, and I uttered these words, which still haunt my very existence. "Just as the sun sets and the moon will surely rise, my life has been filled with the knowledge that I was never meant to be. While it is true that one day my life will end, my pain exists in the hearts of men. I was forced into this world and never understood the

24

point of it all. I know just as the sun comes up, it will surely go down, and it all appears rather pointless.

"I know that no matter what I do, I will find a way to be happy, and that the quest is normally more fulfilling than the goal itself. But when the sun goes down, I'm still alone, with no real home, no real family, no real friends to call my own. As the moon rises, I generally find ways to make sense of a day that ended, with nothing more than me standing around with my dick in my hand. Now it's true, I could go off and find a nice girl, but I've known the pain of love. The pleasure of depression is that you tell yourself that you're better off alone than with the pain. The man that said, 'It's better to have loved and lost than to never have loved at all,' was a fool.

"When I lose something, I tend to try to find it, no matter the cost, no matter the time. I can't sit idly by and do nothing, as I have lost my very will to live; I must go out and hunt it down. Just as the moon falls and the sun reappears in the morning, I know that I must find that which I have lost. Why? Because it haunts my dreams at night, and this is why I reside in a state of constant misery."

The tears were mounting in the eyes of those who heard the pain in my voice, as I described the search for that which I had lost.

Lilly asked, "What was it that you lost?"

I looked her in the eyes and said, "Happiness. I can't really explain it, but I can't recall the last time I was genuinely happy, to the point that I question whether I had ever really been happy."

Now I could see the heads start to shake, and Lilly gave me a hug and proceeded to attach herself to my arm. Mark asked, "Why bother searching?"

I explained that, "The thrill of the hunt is what makes my life worthwhile, so I just keep on moving, like a cowboy in search of a perfect bottle and a nice trail."

He explained why they drift on the river. It wasn't thrill-seeking, but a journey to find something more. I agreed that life just seems like flat soda most of the time, and even if I had never drank a soda, I would still find a flat one to be worthless. That was just how I felt about life. Even though I was wandering around, I still hadn't even come close to what seemed like a good place to squat, and that just bothered me.

Lilly kept stroking my hair and beard, like David playing the harp before the Lord. I could tell she was just trying to get to know me, in the kind of way that one chimpanzee searches another for ticks.

It was around this point that Mark informed me that there was indeed room for one more on the raft, if I wanted to call it home for a while. I decided that while I've never been a fan of drifting, I could give it a try. Why not? I had nothing better to do, and I asked if I could make one quick stop first to grab my last jug of white lightning I left back at my campsite.

Lilly ventured off the raft with me, as I attempted to retrace my steps to find my stuff. We got lost, and it was getting late, so I said, "It's ok, I don't need it that bad. Let's just go."

Lilly suggested that we stay and watch the stars. Who was I to argue? Alas, I knew this would be another reason for my heart to ache, but I couldn't bear the thought of hurting poor Lilly. I tried to tell her I was no good.

I asked her about life on the river, and from what I gathered, there was a lot of fishing, smoking, drinking, and just good old fun. Depending on the river, there was even some bartering going on. I myself was always partial to the barter system, because most of the time it made more sense than swapping around worthless pieces of paper. Life on the river sounded good, and Lilly was smoking hot, so I decided to go for the gold. The next morning, I boarded the raft with my boombox and the clothes on my back.

The next week felt like a dream, just us floating down a peaceful river, smoking, a little drinking, and lots of Tom Foolery. We did some fishing and all that jazz. We hit a patch of the river that led to another river, and like that, we were on the Big Muddy (that's the Mississippi River for you Yankees reading this). We pulled up next to another boat, and we offered them some fish and green for some beer and burgers. It was nice, and I even bummed a pack of Camels.

It was the dream for me: I was working on my tan, and while my body was nothing spectacular, I didn't feel weird going around naked. Nobody seemed to care, and pretty soon the rest of the band of merry fools were naked, too. There we were, floating down river, naked, listening to Hall and Oates, smoking joints, and grilling some fish. I was in Heaven for all of the next ten minutes, until a barge came up on the horizon. I looked up and saw the ripple on the river coming our way. That big wake hit our dinky raft, and then we were swimming for the shore.

I managed to grab Lilly and a rope that was holding our vessel together. Once ashore, we weren't quite sure what to do: the raft was upside down and the head count was off. We were short one girl, Monica, who wasn't to be seen or heard from. I went under the raft in the water for a peek, but she wasn't there. I looked around and saw a log in the middle of the river, so I made my way out, carrying the rope in one hand. Swimming wasn't really an option: it was more or less just flailing my feet up and out, while trying not to get stabbed by the floating hypodermics.

I finally got to the log, and there was Monica. Sure, she was all hot, wet, naked, and confused, but she was still breathing, so I grabbed her, and we made it back to shore. Mark and Harry looked very upset. I figured by the way they were looking at the ice chest floating its merry way down river that the weed was gone, and they didn't look too happy. Harry was cussing up a storm, and Mark was biting his knuckles.

I walked up, and Harry said, "This is all your fault!" Mark said that he blamed me for ruining his dream. I was a little confused, naked, still stoned, and very wet. I had cut my hand on the rope. I figured, hey, at least the raft was intact. I found a way to flip it back over and tied it to the shore while everything was drying.

The boys were still fighting, and they weren't very laid back anymore. I suggested that maybe we could catch up to the ice chest, but I was told to shut up and get off the raft. I feared I was about to marooned on the banks of the Mississippi.

Lilly and Monica decided to get off the raft and sit with me. They were trying to console me, reminding me that I had saved her. I wasn't exactly crying, but more or less trying to get my land legs back under me, physically and emotionally. That's when Jennifer quietly untied the boat, as Mark and Harry were busy talking. She whistled to me, and that's when Lilly and Monica grabbed me.

The next thing I knew, I was drifting on the river with all three girls, and the two pissed off yuppies were cussing and screaming at us from the shore. I knew that Hell had a special place for Mutineers, Thieves, and Yuppies. I figured, "Oh, well, sucks to be them."

As I looked ahead, I noticed the ice chest was caught up on the bank just a little further down. We made our way over to it. Success! It was full, and I also found a six pack of PBR that Mark had been hiding. I felt weird leaving them behind, but the women decided it was going to end like that. I was cool with their decision, and we started where we left off, just minus two.

Unfortunately, the boombox was gone, swallowed by the unforgiving waters. As much as I wanted to feel bad, I knew it was all good. For once in my life, things were going good. It wasn't long until our clothes were dry, and the tent was shredded, but oh well. I cracked open the PBR and laid back, gazing at the sky. Lilly and Monica opted to lie beside me. Jennifer started crying, but moments later she lay down behind me and let me use her body as a pillow.

She then began to list everything wrong that Mark and Harry had ever done. After this had gone on for twenty minutes, I couldn't take all the negativity, so I told her, "They're behind us, forget about it," but she wouldn't let it go. Then Monica began to make her own list, and Lilly joined in the mix. It was like Hell on a raft, but along with the bitching and whining, I was getting massaged and smoking herb. I figured that this would work, so I just nodded my head, agreeing with whatever they said.

Now despite the joy of being the only guy in a group of four naked people drifting down the river, the Mississippi was hell-bent on making our voyage miserable. She kept throwing eddies our way, and it made relaxing a bit tough. It also made the sex rather interesting.

In between the sex, smoking, and river guiding, I found a way to figure out where we were. Using my evasive Magic Ninja-orienteering skills, I deduced we were about 18 miles north of Vicksburg. It wasn't long before I was letting my mind wander as to what should be done next.

Night Journey
By JT Davenport

(Editor's note: according to JT Davenport, the following is a true story. You be the judge.)

I never imagined these things to be real, and as such, I never bothered to even think about them past the point of, "That's pure fantasy and folk tales; most certainly could never happen." I mean, just how can you justify being dead, but not dead at the same time? It defies explanation and is not scientifically possible. Well, all of that notwithstanding, just how then do you explain vampirism? We've seen in the movies and in books that ALL vampires are EVIL. Well, if that's so, then how do you explain the GOLDEN ONES?!

I had not one, but two questions I couldn't explain. You see, I was driving home one night at about 3 am. I don't exactly remember which day it was, and that truly isn't important for the story. As I recall, I was on the interstate, driving my van and singing along with the music on the radio, when this idiot driver lost control of his car on the rain-slick roadway and veered directly in front of me. I had no choice but to yank hard to the right on the steering wheel and hope there was no one in the far right lane. Luckily there wasn't.

Perhaps it might have been better for me if there had been someone driving in that lane, since I ended up hitting one of the underpass pylons with the right front of the van. The impact ripped the seatbelt loose and threw me through the windshield. After I flew thirty feet through the air and landed in one of those grassy areas at the cloverleaf turnoffs, I knew what tenderized hamburger meat felt like after the tenderizing had been done! I was sliced up, had broken many bones, and was bleeding profusely. I figured I wasn't going to make it to sunrise. Thankfully, I was numb and free of pain.

As I lay there on the grass, I fancied I saw something...LARGE. It looked like a huge, glowing bird spiraling down to the ground. "Geez," I thought, "why did I get this damn bird to carry me to wherever we go when we die, when I could have had a Valkyrie?!" I sort of fancied Brunhilda, coming to sweep me up in her iron-clad bosom! Then again, perhaps the bird was going to eat me right here, in front of all of the people driving on the interstate.

After it landed next to me, I thought I was hallucinating. Then this great big, golden, glowing bird started talking to me. No, not out loud, but in my mind. I know, that's so much more normal, right?

"We have been watching you for a good while, and I now have an offer for you. If you want, you can be healed and live, or you can die," she calmly stated.

I didn't know exactly what to think, but if this was a hallucination, it was a pretty damned good one. Still, she did seem to be very serious and was apparently waiting for an answer. What kind of an answer does anyone give to a question like that? I mean, just how often do you have a traffic accident that throws you through a windshield and lets you land on the grass where you can die, and then suddenly a giant golden eagle that sort of glows lands next to you and telepathically talks to you? My guess is not every day. I thought I was mad.

"If you want to be saved, you must choose right now. You don't have long to live," she said, a bit impatiently.

"Ok, ok, I'll play along with this," I thought. "Uhmm, I do have a few questions to ask before choosing," I stated. Off in the distance, I could hear the sound of several sirens wailing their way slowly closer to me.

"First, why me, and second, are you evil?" I asked in my most matter of fact manner.

"We don't have time for this! YOU ARE DYING. NOW CHOOSE!" she said.

"Not yet. Answer my questions first."

"Alright, if I must. First, you were recommended to us, and second, NO, we are not evil! Now choose," she said flatly.

"Ok, then I choose to live," was all I said.

In the next instant, it seemed as if the great eagle sort of melted into me. In that same moment, I could feel my broken bones mending, my blood returning to my body, and all the damage being healed!

It felt like only a minute passed before I could stand up, and as I did so, the EMTs and the police showed up, and all sorts of questions got asked. They were incredulous that my clothes were so shredded and bloody, but I didn't have a scratch on me! I felt great!

I told them what happened (minus the part about glowing owls), and after about a million questions, I got to go home. The police gave me a ride to my house, and my van got towed to a repair shop. I thanked the officer and headed up the walkway to the front door. All the time I was thinking I'd had some sort of weird hallucination. I was thanking God for being fortunate enough to have not been as seriously hurt as I thought I'd been.

As I played it back in my head on the walk up, it seemed that I had managed to bust through the windshield without getting cut and landed on the grass without breaking any bones. The police and the EMTs were at a complete loss on how to explain this one, and I told them I was just as perplexed. Well, all I wanted was to get a long, hot shower and curl up in bed for a long night's sleep.

I remember being awakened the next morning by someone talking to me. It sounded like a female, but I had gone to sleep by myself. It must be my imagination playing tricks on me again. I chose to ignore it and rolled over to sleep some more, but I didn't get to close my eyes this time.

"I said, 'GOOD MORNING'!" she loudly stated. And there, on my carpet, was that huge golden eagle. "I have a lot of things to tell you in order to get you ready and not a lot of time to do it in. So please, listen up." As she cleared her throat to begin her speech or talk, I interrupted.

"Just what in the hell are you and why are you hounding me? Oh God, I must be going...no, check that: I must have gone insane, because this simply cannot be happening! Aw, jeez, what are the shrinks going to think about this? I'll bet they haven't hea-"

"SHUT UP NOW, AND LISTEN TO WHAT I HAVE TO TELL YOU, or else I'll return you to the damaged thing I found on the grass last night!" she impatiently interrupted my musings.

"Do you mean you're real, and I'm NOT making all of this up?" I asked, looking straight at her.

There's nothing like staring down a giant bird of prey that's sitting on your bedroom carpet to bring you fully awake. You begin to appreciate the few options you really have, as I scanned my bedroom for an effective weapon to defend myself with, if I had to. None of the guns in my bedroom were loaded. (Mental note to self: LOAD THEM NEXT TIME!) All I had within reach was a very sharp Arkansas toothpick.

"Now listen, please."

With those words, my education began.

It all got started in an old Cherokee legend, and more than a few other nations have this legend as well. It's the legend of the Bird Tribe and the Golden Ones. According to the legend, the Bird Tribe came from the sky and helped to create humans and other things on this planet (ie: they were extraterrestrials).

I've never told you or, for that matter, anyone else about one of my very lucid dreams. I can have these dreams even when awake, so long as my eyes are closed. It's like watching a movie screen on the back of my eyelids. I will still be alert to my surroundings and can hear clearly what is going on around me, but if my eyes are closed, I'm NOT seeing the backside of them! I place these "dreams" in a totally different category from all of the other dream types. They are so extremely vivid it is sometimes hard to tell them from reality.

Here's one of them. I remember looking out from where I was standing and seeing an Indian tree, which was bent so it would overlook a very green valley. On the other side of the Indian tree was the Mississippi River. In this valley was a Wal-Mart, complete with asphalt parking lot. I moved to the building by the power of thought and entered it in the same way.

Upon entering, I took a moment to orient myself and get my bearings. I suddenly realized there was a robbery going on, and I was about twenty feet behind two black men with shotguns, who were attempting to hold up the store. I had one of my katanas with me.

Suddenly, something was behind me, just to my left, and it was taller than I was by a head. Its head was also very dark, blackish even. Without thinking, I whipped the katana out of my sheath and neatly cut the head off the creature.

I then picked up the head. It was that of a black raven's head, except human-sized, and for some reason, I began drinking its blood, which was pouring out of the severed head. I drained it to the last drop.

I recall having the oddest sensation: it was like I was supposed to have done that, because now Raven was inside me, a part of me in a way you could never get by any other method.

Well, the black guys must have seen or heard something, because they began to turn towards me. It was like they were in slow motion, which really meant I had sped up. I was probably using the Void again, that all-powerful force true masters of the arcane can know, because this is one of the things that happens when you use that element.

The two black men were beginning to raise their shotguns in my direction, when I raised one of my hands and two fireballs shot outwards, one after the other. They flew straight towards the two would-be robbers, hitting each of them in the chest. They flew backwards like two broken puppets and landed on the floor. They didn't move.

Ever since then I've been able to do certain things from time to time, and I'm beginning to think the dream was intended to allow Raven into my head. I now know what my two totems are. These I randomly drew from a deck of Indian medicine cards, although I already knew which ones they were going to be and said as much to one of my friends who was there at the time. I picked Raven and Snake out of the deck, and in that order! Raven is on my female side, and Snake is on my male side. I knew that dream was prophetic. Since then, I have carried them with me on the inside.

But I digress. The Golden Ones were made by the spirit of the world, that vibrant, life-giving force in a moment of lucidity, and they were intended to combat the monsters born out of evil entering the world. As all manner of evils sprang forth from Pandora's Box, the Golden Ones were a sight better than just some hope at the bottom of a box! They are NOT evil. Yes, they do drink blood, but unlike other vampires, only from animals. They have a herd of cattle that they collect blood from, store it, and drink it when needed. They do have human and animal helpers that they share some of their power with to assist them in their tasks.

There are only five of the Golden Ones. There's Zincala, the oldest and wisest of us all. Zincala has power likened unto a demigod, like a Hercules. He looks like a whip-thin, Apache Indian male with pale blue eyes, except he's much older than the Apache Indian tribe.

The rest of us are mightier than mere mortal men and can live forever, but our powers would be more like that of a blessed warrior saint, who could battle dragons and demons without fear. When we sit in council, we sit as in a sacred circle: North, East, South and West, including one in the center. There is a female who sits in the North: her color is golden white, and she has a huge owl as her bird-form. I sit in the East, my color is golden yellow (of all things), and my bird-form is a huge eagle. He who sits in the South is colored blue and has a huge hawk eagle as his bird-form. He who sits in the West is colored red, and his bird-form is a huge bald eagle. The one in the center, Zincala, bears all of these colors, and his bird-form is a huge harpy eagle.

From this circle, we chant and affect many things by doing so. As bird-people, we can do special things, and as vampires, we can do other things as well. We take an avid interest in the goings on of the evil vampires and other evils that haunt the world.

Of the evils we track, all use the Memphis area as a feeding ground, including vampires and werewolves (why did you think Memphis was so violent?!), but they normally get along, so long as each's turf and territory are respected. Then there are the outsiders, like the voodoo people and the Satanists, who don't get along with anybody. There are a few sorcerers from the ancient societies and mystical fraternities that tend to mind their own business.

You can find several other creatures of note in the Memphis area. There are the wolfen, which is a small pack of five wolves who were once Native Americans who emulated wolves as they hunted. They did this so well that they became wolves themselves and gained the ability to transform themselves from human to wolf at will. They actively hunt evil of any kind in the Memphis area, too. A mummy also got loose when the Ramses exhibit came through town, because it thought it was home and that the time had come to start a new empire!

There is a supernatural council called Parliament, which meets beneath the current downtown Memphis in Old Memphis, in an abandoned church buried beneath the new city all the tourists and residents know. In the underground, you'll find revenants, zombies, ghosts, and other odd creatures, plus some strange people who live down there. There is even a tunnel made entirely of yellow bricks, and no one knows who built the tunnel or how long ago it was built. They don't even know where it goes! This tunnel has been locked up by the city.

I guess my education was taking longer than she thought, or else I'm just a slow learner, because what I thought was going to take only a few minutes ended up taking hours. I was hungry and wanted to take a shower and a good shit, and not necessarily in that order. So I held my hand up and said so.

The big bird moved aside, and as I passed, I resisted the urge to pluck a feather or two, fearing for my own safety and welfare. I then walked into the bathroom and began to close the door, but the damned bird kept coming on right behind me. It entered the bathroom and just stood there, waiting.

Ok, enough is enough, and I've had it with this damned big bird! Hell's bells, I didn't like Big Bird on Sesamie Street, so why should I like this version of it? It was time to tell this owl a thing or two!

"Alright, enough is enough! I'm going to take a shower, a shit, and a pee! Hell, I might even shave if I feel like it, but I'm going to do them ALONE! Now get out, and that means NOW!" I shouted.

"I thought I made it very clear: we cannot be separated by as much as ten feet, or both of us will die now," the big bird stated flatly.

"Then you can just sit outside of the door and wait, because you are NOT going to sit there and watch! Now, get out!" With that, I slammed the bathroom door in the face of the big bird and locked it! I felt a rush of confidence and satisfaction surge over me as I did this, a sense of accomplishment that just wouldn't stop.

After my tithe to Porcellana, the Goddess of the Swirling Waters, had been completed, I jumped into the shower and lathered up. While this was going on, I began singing the words to "The Bridge over the River Kwai". I can sometimes be sadistic, and I just wanted to rub it in some more, so I sang:

> HITLER HAS ONLY GOT ONE BALL
> GOERING'S GOT TWO, BUT THEY ARE SMALL
> HIMMLER'S ARE RATHER SIMILAR
> AND GOEBBELS HASN'T GOT ONE AT ALL!

I did this over and over for at least thirty minutes, maybe longer. I enjoyed it, I must admit.

When it came time to finally get out of the shower, I carefully peeked out past the shower curtain. There in the middle of the bathroom floor calmly sat the big bird, not moving, except for the little rivulets of water cascading off its body and landing on the bathroom floor. Damn it, one of the things I cherish the most is my privacy, and I also do my best to give that same respect back to others. The door was still shut, and I got angrier by the second.

So I went over to the door, unlocked it and ordered that damn owl out! "GET THE HELL OUT NOW, AND NEVER DO THAT AGAIN! DID YOU HEAR ME?! OUT!"

"But I almost died!" she said pleadingly.

"But you didn't!" I replied. "And, what's more, you'll get really good at almost dying each and every morning, and each and every time I need to go to the can," I shouted.

This time, I merely raised my right hand and pointed towards the door, my silent demand being obvious.

"But, but..." the big bird stammered. With that, she wobbled out of the door, leaving the cloud of steam that was still in the bathroom.

I triumphantly slammed the door and turned on the fan to get rid of the steam cloud. I shaved and put on some aftershave, then walked out still wrapped in a towel, feeling rather smug. I next moved into the master bedroom and collected the clothes I was going to wear that day. The great bird closely followed, although it did look a good bit ragged.

I returned to the bathroom, closed the door and began to dress as quickly as I could. As I turned off the fan, I heard something hit the floor outside in the hallway, so I opened the bathroom door quickly and stepped out into the hallway.

There on the floor, in an awkward position, was slumped the great bird. "Well, at least it had the decency to die quietly," I thought. "Ah, but that doesn't seem to be the case now does it? Hell no, I'm still alive, and that means it is, too."

I nudged it with my left foot and noticed a slight stirring coming from it, followed by a rapid flutter of wings. It stood up and shook itself into alertness. "Look, toots, I happen to be a person who REALLY likes his personal privacy, and you're going to have to get some sort of divine intervention that will allow you to be further away from me, or else you're going to go through this scene each and every morning. I sometimes hop into the shower three to four times a day. Anyway, like I told you, you wouldn't die by being apart from me the distance you were, see?" I calmly mocked, as I crossed my arms across my chest and looked at the big bird.

"By the way, do you have any other form you can change into? It is going to seem rather odd to those who will now see me leaving my house being closely followed by a giant bird. Imagine for a moment the startled looks on those people who would be driving past my house and saw what I just described. Now imagine what the police dispatcher would think if someone were to actually call it in to the police station. Imagine what it's going to look like to people who will see us pass them in my truck? There I'll be driving, and they'll see this huge bird perched on the right front passenger seat doing it's very best to look ordinary. It just ain't going to work," I tried to point out.

All she could say was, "But, but…"

"Further, imagine how I'm going to explain all of the feathers, which are illegal to own, being in my house. This means I can't even throw them away, because the garbage men will report me. Then I'll go to jail, and later on I'll go to prison. And I'm certain you wouldn't last very long in lockup, which is where they'd put me along with other guys in one cell. Do you really think they're going to ignore the fact that you would be in the cell? HELL NO, they wouldn't. They'd shoot you or put you in a cell by yourself, until they consulted with the governor or someone else in authority. There, you see the problems you're causing now?!

"And, I really don't like being a mule for some neo-version of a voodoo deity, either!" I pointed out. "Of course, if you were to change into a gorgeous babe instead of a female version of Big Bird, it would be a whole lot better, but NOOOOOOOOO! You can't do that, can you, because that would be too simple? What do I get saddled with? A living version of Big Bird, that's what! And now, everywhere I go, the little kids will be yelling, 'Oh mommy, there goes Big Bird!' Or, I'll have restaurant owners coming out, saying something like this, 'I'm sorry, sir, but, we don't allow giant birds in our restaurant. You'll have to put it on a perch and leave it chained outside.'

"Or, even more interesting, imagine how I'm going to feel walking into any of my local grocery stores and having the managers come up to me and say, 'You're going to have to leave IT outside, because IT's making the customers nervous!' Are you finally getting my point?! And of course, there'll be those sport hunters who'll be shooting at you, since you'd be the keystone of stuffed animal heads they've shot and killed. Now imagine that!"

"But, you said you were willing to-"

I stopped her in mid-sentence and retorted with, "Sugar, anyone who was dying would have said and done the same things I did. I appreciate the fact that you saved my life, but I am a living human being, and I do need my space, even more of it than others. And since I've now tried that mule-thing about hosting you inside my body, I can tell you this: I really don't like that at all."

She quietly stated that what I said was not quite right. "By now, the change should be complete, which means you are technically now dead and should be officially listed as undead. As such, you can no longer eat what you used to. So you might as well start getting used to drinking blood."

41

Oh, great, another bump in the road. "Look, I hate to tell you this, but ever since I used to work in research, I have been allergic to other creatures' blood, and that includes other humans as well. It causes me to swell up like a balloon, and when that happens, I have trouble breathing," I fired back at her. "I can't help that, but it's the truth. Now, who do we have to see to get this straightened out?" I asked quietly, in a more resigned voice.

"I guess we need to speak with Zincala, the head of our group," was all she said.

We drove for a good forty-five minutes to an hour before we got to the Munford/Atoka area. This is the fiefdom, so to speak, of the Golden Ones. We eventually got to see Zincala, who was, as usual, very busy tending to things.

"Sir, we have a problem, and we don't know how to fix this. The problem is this: she can't be even a few feet away from me, and this is driving me nuts. I'm the kind of person who likes to go to the bathroom for a dump and a good pee by myself. I really don't like being watched by a very large bird of prey while I'm sitting on the toilet. She can't even be just outside the bathroom in the hallway without nearly dying, and this is not good for either one of us," I stated in as plain a way as I thought was possible.

"Yes," she said. "I don't see how this is going to work out, unless there is some sort of accommodation we can make." It was more of a plea, because you could tell she was just as miserable about this problem as I was.

All Zincala said was, "We'll see how to solve this problem, rest assured. Now, please get ready for tonight's ritual ceremony."

Tonight, we were going to reinforce the barrier that has been keeping the Leshyia, our wayward cousins, on the western side of the Mississippi. Each of us had to put on our body paint and dress attire. We'd be dancing before long, and after that we'd be taking pot shots at those evil things that go bump in the night once again.

I was painted in yellow and sat in the East of the sacred circle. The others were painted according to where they would sit in that same circle. We danced into the middle hours of the night, and then we departed from the circle after the closing invocations were finished. From there, we quickly prepared to take flight and go after some evil things and bump back all night long. We knew we'd be making the entire area that much safer once we were through.

The Runner
By Stephen Clements and JT Davenport

Maria Conchita Sanchez is a hot, phat-ass Latina chica; she's also a wallet-grabbing whore. This is her story, and how she made the world a better place.

"Sup, baby?" asked Jatarius, his ebony skin gleaming with sweat under the bloated California sun. He was leaned back against his tricked-out ghetto sled, his propped up Air Force One's carelessly scuffing the paint job.

Maria smiled coyly at Jatarius, walking slowly toward him in her platform sandals, making sure her smooth, caramel legs lustered just right all the way up to her booty-hugging short skirt. She'd done this before to wannabe ballers with ice slung around their neck and platinum spinners that cost more than the car they were put on. She knew those poor sacks didn't even have to look above her waist to gladly lose all their cash to her.

Let's face it: it's not hard to convince short guys who like to flex to drop some bread on hot bitches for some ass. Maria's problem was that she had plenty of ass, not so much cash. Before you condemn her for prostitution, just know that Maria prefers to think of it as theft with an appetizer of skeezy sex. It really works for both of them: supply and demand, yo. It's all like economics up in this bitch.

Jatarius bit his bottom lip when he smiled, his whole face lighting up with the treat coming closer to him. He stood up and moved aside, opening the heavy door for the lady. She smiled and looked up at him, as she helped herself into the purple, fuzzy passenger seat.

When the car door shut, she made a quick survey of the hooptie she found herself in. The shiny beads hanging from the rear-view mirror were just plastic: not worth shit. The chrome

8-ball knob on the gear shift was obviously fake: no point in taking that. The windows were rolled down, so she doubted if this guy could afford to run the air conditioner: she'd have to be careful with this one. She knew she could kick his ass if she had to, but she didn't want to give away any of the goods to a broke bitch.

So Jatarius got Maria in his caddy, and they cruised on down the Strip. See, he had to set the stage, get the proper ambiance to tell her how much money he had and how good he'd be to her, if she'd just let him up in that thang. He told her some tired lines about how special she was and how he was falling for her already, and that he'd show her how good it was to be with a real gangsta. Like he told all the other girls who hate his guts now.

Good thing for Maria was that he was so hopped up on the smell of his own shit, he had no clue that he was about to be had. She let him talk, listened so intently, and knew just when and how to say, "Oh baby, you drivin' me crazy!" She had learned how to make this soft moan that said both "I love you" and "You feel so good inside me" that made every man melt. Maria might have problems, but a conscience ain't one.

But like Hell she was gonna give it up in this hood rat's car. She knew if they got nasty in his car, when he got done, he'd just drop her off somewhere, wink a kiss at her, and say he'd call her later. No cash.

As she gently stroked his ear, she cooed, "Baby, take me someplace special. I wants to do nasty tings wit' you. I want to ruin some clean sheets wit' you."

"It was in the bag," he thought. "Aight, baby, is cool," he said. "There's a party going on later, at muh boy's house. I chill wif him all da time, up in the Hills. It's gonna get freaky, though: my boy makes them movies wif da hoochies gettin' it good. He's down. I smoke him up all da time."

Now this was much better: if Jatarius doesn't pay up, there will be plenty of other guys to shake-down there.

Jatarius drove Maria in his ghetto chariot to the magical palace of the porn king when the sun retired from the sky. After the guard at the white gate checked them through, all seemed well, and they were greeted by the sight of three naked blondes being chased by one of the kingpin's studs, jiggling their impossibly perfect proportions all the way. The green lawn was covered in blankets and games played by people, who even in their decadence were far more respectable than Maria or her meal ticket. Good: less competition. These bitches will throw it away for free.

A tastefully sun-kissed white man with gray hair walked down the marble steps to the driveway, his perfectly creased white suit massaging him as he went. He smiled at the pair as he raised his right hand in salutation. "Jermaine, so good to see you! How are you tonight? And who is this delightful beauty you have with you?" he asked, moving his hand to take Maria's lotioned hand in his.

Jatarius took the wrong name in stride and answered, "Yo, John, this is my new girl Maria. I think she might be the one," he said, his greasy smile spreading.

John the pornographer retorted, "If he doesn't happen to be your one, please let me know. I'd like to fill out my application for the job." He smiled as he pecked the back of her hand tastefully, and the look in his eyes made Maria relax. She knew he was a predator, because he made his millions by having the insides of young women dogged out for the amusement of countless anonymous people around the world. But his eyes were beautiful, and she didn't get the feeling that he was sizing her up for market. He was a wolf, but this one couldn't eat another bite.

"So nice to meet you, John. You have a beautiful home," she greeted him right back. Sometimes Maria dreamt of having a place like this for herself. She knew better than to make a go at John and try to take his, though: he would devour her and leave nothing for her to keep. She knew how to run a racket, but his game operated on a level she knew she couldn't compete on.

But every other guy here would be a lesser man, and she would fuck them up for breakfast.

"Well, thank you, Maria. But there's so much more to see! Come along you two, let me show you around and get you something to drink," John said, leading them through the gleaming doors. And so the old wolf charmed, and the young huntress watched, ever fearful that the master would take his prey.

After a few drinks and lines of blow, though, everybody was everybody's best friend. Maria played her part, charming in her own turn as they went, sizing up the gentlemen here, and she and John even promised to work together someday. She drove a bargain, even as she had no intention of keeping it.

But she remembered what she came here for: snatch Jatarius' bling and get the hell out. For those concerned about the wannabe hustler's feelings, he got what he wanted, too. That night, Jatarius and Maria, like a newlywed royal couple, got snowed, drank, and fucked for hours.

At the end of their entirely one-sided coital bliss, her man of the day lay passed out on the ruined, formerly white sheets after screaming his own name. There was no attempt at cuddling; the sounds of their love-making had gone silent, being replaced by the thumping of the disco music below. Maria lay still on top of the sheets, her naked candy skin beaded with his sweat. When his snores began to rattle the walls, she took that as her signal to get to work.

She didn't get dressed right away: that might tip off anybody who caught her digging around. Step one: check his pants. Maria rifled through his stubby, dirty jeans. Nothing worth having. They already did the drugs he had in there.

Step two: check his unbuttoned, plaid shirt. A half-smoked joint. Nothing again. Shit. So he said this is the room he stays in sometimes.

Step three: check the drawers. Okay, loose change, lambskin condoms, lube, an Old Testament, rolling papers, some little, blue pills.

Nightstand one down, now nightstand two. "Finally!" her mind thrilled at the find. Okay, platinum, diamonds, wallet-clipped rolls of bills, cocaine. Good. Time to grab and go.

Maria grabbed up her purse, keeping her hands steady with the force of mind learned from having to be functional when her drug-addled body would rather go wild. A true professional knows how to operate under any condition. In two quick swipes, Maria emptied the drawer into her purse. The resonating snores continued, assuring Maria that her mark was blissfully oblivious to the thousands of dollars this piece of ass just cost him.

This was a good night, the wildly unfulfilling sex notwithstanding. And she wasn't worried about John possibly getting upset by her stealing in his house. He was a fucking pervert and could burn in Hell.

Maria quickly pulled the rest of her clothes onto her tight body without bothering to tame her frazzled black hair. As she stalked out of the white marble and crystal mansion, she pulled out her tiny, pink cell phone to call a taxi. On her way through the den, she noticed that the entire floor was covered with a blanketing of fluffy pillows and party animals, who had passed out where they'd fallen. The two dozen people lay in various

48

states of dress and undress, coitus and non-coitus. Halfway across the room, she was startled by a sudden noise.

"Hey, mama," weakly called one of Jatarius' hood friends, as he lay helpless on an overstuffed couch. His bleary eyes had only registered something female moving, not even having the strength to look at her. Even if he were sober, it'd take him ten minutes to get out of that much cushion. The best he could manage now was, "Where you goin'? Wi-onch you give me a tickle, mama?"

Maria just looked over her shoulder and smiled, not having any more time to waste on these punk bitches. As she made it out onto the still perfectly-kept grass, the operator picked up on the other end. "Hola, Felici Taxi."

"Hola, necessito un taxi."

It wasn't so much that Maria had gotten enough rest and was ready to wake up, as it was that her cousin Gabriela's cupboards were really loud and always slammed shut when closed. No matter how you tried to ease it down, it snapped that last inch and could piss off the dead. Gabriela wasn't the kind to care about that.

Maria started moving, slowly, propping herself up on her elbows as her puffy eyes struggled to open. She could tell it was about noon, from the light of the sun coming through the beige towel placed over the high, long window running the length of the living room wall. Maria hadn't had a place of her own to call home in years, but Gabriela let her stay on the couch in her one-bedroom. It's small, but it's shelter.

Her cousin walked into the living room in her tank top and wrinkly, pink shorts, her chubby thighs trembling while she carried an oversized bowl of cereal over to the love-seat. The television clicked on hesitantly.

"What time is it?" Maria asked weakly.

"Tree-tirty," Gabriela said, as she crunched the multi-colored sugary eats without pause.

Still groggy, Maria moved the worn, grungy blanket off her and stood to walk to the bathroom. She felt all the nastiness of last night clinging to her like scum on a dirty sink. Her head pounded, and she was sore, in some places not remembering why.

She was lost in the misery of her head throbbing violently, when a loud thumping came on the screen door at the far end of the kitchen. Maria groaned and walked to the bathroom, hoping for the thin walls to take the edge off whatever obnoxious vatho was at the apartment door. She snatched her purse for the lotion she kept in there, to ease her troubled skin.

Maria closed the door to the small bathroom and held herself up over the sink. She needed to be steady now. She didn't turn on the lights, because the weak light coming through the frosted window hurt enough as it was. The bathroom was all done in white, so it would light up miserably if she turned it on.

She heard muffled voices at the door; apparently, Gabriela decided to see who the asshole was. Figuring it wasn't any of her problem, Maria grabbed a hand towel and reached over to turn on the cold water and get about her business. Then the voices got louder.

"Lis-en, you can't talk to me like dat. Dis is my 'ouse, so you need to geet on," Gabriela chastised.

"I AIN'T TELLIN' YO' ILLEGAL ASS AGAIN, BITCH! WHERE IS THE 'HO AT?"

"Oh, no you di-int! You need to – AHHH!" Gabriela's cry pierced the air.

Maria looked up, her eyes staring back into her blood-shot orbs in the mirror. What the hell was happening?

Two loud pops clarified the matter, and then a crash as the screen door was smashed in.

"Oh, my God, Gabriela! Oh, my God, what happened?!" Maria whispered to herself, suddenly terrified.

As she heard heavy stomps enter the living room from the kitchen, her left hand automatically locked the bathroom door, seemingly on its own accord. She didn't think it, her body just did it. She knew she couldn't leave the bathroom to find out what had happened to Gabriela right now. She had a sick feeling in her stomach that she already knew.

But fuck it. Grabbing her purse, she reached over to the frosted, white window and pulled the latch to open it as far as it would go. The hot, dry air rushed in on her from the outside, the sun hurting her panic-widened eyes.

With the window swinging to its widest point, Maria slipped out, her flesh squeezed as she pulled through. Her soft hands felt the bite of the white plaster on the side of the apartment, but paid it no mind. The jiggling of the locked door handle gave her all the incentive she needed to not care about such a petty, transient thing as pain.

She hit the rough concrete and scrambled to keep moving. A kick at the bathroom door reverberated out of the room, and the violence behind it carried its full weight to Maria's ears. Her eyes darted around, looking for someplace to hide for a moment, but fuck this neighborhood: there's nothing big enough for her to hide behind!

Another kick at the flimsy door convinced her it was time to just run. Damn it if they shot her in the back in the open: she could take a chance, or have no chance at all. The door crashed open behind her, and she heard the angry cursing as her hunters entered the room.

Three hoodlums were hot on her trail, her bare feet carrying her quickly away from the slow thugs, who were struggling to pull up their sagging pants as they chased after her. The pursuit was intense, as every step, every breath that flew in and out of her lungs moved through her mind like a stop-and-go slideshow. Maria's mind analyzed every second, to see which way to run, to check if there was a way out, and bracing for the impact of a round finding its mark and knocking her to the pavement. They had been chasing her for blocks when she decided to cut a corner, thinking she had enough of a lead to be able to disappear.

Turning the corner, she saw a wide open boulevard in the hard sunlight, and no other corners she could dodge past to give them the slip. The few open shops had almost completely glass storefronts, offering her no concealment from their eyes.

But there was a dumpster on the side of the road. With all the adrenaline coursing through her veins, she vaulted into the giant box and pulled the lid down over her. In the dumpster, the only sound she could hear was her heavy breathing echoing hollow in the grimy container. It took a few moments for her to become aware of the dull roar of the garbage truck trundling towards her. A fresh, new panic gripped her insides, as she felt the dumpster being lifted into the air, and her and the fetid contents slipping and rotating towards the back of the truck. She clawed desperately for any hand-hold to grip in the container, but joined the slop in the bed of the truck anyway.

"To Hell with those guys and their damn guns," she thought, as she furiously scrambled her way up to get out of the truck bed before it compacted her to become one with the wet cigarette butts and half empty Diet Coke bottles. She pulled herself over the tailgate before she was destined to be recycled, the strength and speed borne of a certain death edging ever closer.

Black spots clouded her vision as she landed feet first on the road, and she stumbled back against the truck. As she caught her breath, she saw her pursuers pulling up their pants, walking away. One of the garbage men jogged over to her, his eyes wide in alarm. He asked Maria something in a distant, concerned voice that her mind just didn't care to grasp onto. His words limply pressed against her senses, but found no purchase. She stumbled away from the dump truck, then dizzily walked away from the scene.

Maria called a cab and cussed at the driver to race to her friend Enrico's house, a few better neighborhoods away. She launched herself out of the taxi when she saw the cookie-cutter, pink-brick and poorly landscaped house come into view. It was the late afternoon, and when Enrico saw the glistening piece of hotness that was Maria at his door, he opened it wide.

"Hey, sugar. What brings you by?" Enrico finished, mouthing a silent kiss at her. She said nothing, instead rushing past him, away from the painful rays of the lingering sun.

She looked at him, tears welling in her eyes. "Somebody shot Gabriela."

Enrico wasn't expecting this kind of visit and leaned back, his wife-beater undershirt pulling up to show his mulatto midriff. "Baby, where is this get-together going?"

Tears streaming down her face, she shrieked back the answer, "SOMEBODY SHOT GABRIELA! In the kitchen. Then they came after me."

Enrico let it soak in, hanging his head as he leaned back against the island in his kitchen. "I'm sorry. That booty was fat. I never even got to hit that," he sweetly genuflected. Then it hit him: "So what do they want you for?"

"They wanted me," Maria said, beginning to gesticulate in exasperation. "They came to the house, and they wanted me, but Gabriela got in the way. So they, uh, umm…" she trailed off, as a catch built up in her throat. She slowly slunk down

53

against the wall of the brightly colored kitchen. What had happened back there was starting to sink in, that her cousin, her only real friend, had been murdered.

Gabriela was dead.

With all this news in the open and the unlikelihood that a crying whore is going to put out, Enrico's patience let him know the show was over. Suddenly picking up a very business-like tone, he said, "Well, it's been good to see you! Guess it's time for you to get going."

Reaching down, he took Maria by the elbow and helped raise her back up on her feet and out the door. As she was brought back to reality from her misery, confusion swept over her face. "But where am I supposed to go?" she croaked past the tears and snot working its way down her face.

"I don't know, but I gots to go to work, and you've got a lot to think about, so let me help you get on with the healing process," he continued firmly, as his right hand reached to open the door to the outside world.

As the late afternoon sun worked its way past the door, the smirk that was about to work its way onto Enrico's face got cut short. See, that's when a muffled shot rang out from the street. Crashing through the window, the round left a bloody halo in the middle of Enrico's forehead.

His lanky body slumped and fell over, releasing his unkind grip from Maria's elbow. She screamed as the world went numb, and her instincts took over. Her mind went into a haze, where she could see but didn't see what was in front of her; she made decisions about which way to run, but didn't think it through.

She ran.

Maria ran from L.A. She tried Phoenix, where her aunt and uncle lived. When she cried the news into Uncle Gustavo's chest, the surprise at seeing her at all gave way to sorrow. "Pobrecita," they said. "Of course you can stay here. We're so sorry to hear about Gabriela. This must be very hard on you."

She didn't tell them how Gabriela, her closest family, was gunned down. She fed them some bullshit about Gabriela overdosing on too many pills and leaving a note. She didn't want to find out she was related to more Enricos.

Maria was given the daybed in the sewing room (yeah, this part of the family actually had the money for a whole room to dedicate to sewing, not cramming more people into), and she had her first hot shower in three days. The bus trip here was enough to make her vomit, and there was still the filth from John's party she hadn't washed off herself. Then there was the stain of that punk bitch Jatarius to wash off.

Things weren't going to be easy, but this house was so much nicer than what she was used to. They had central air conditioning, not drippy window units; Aunt Floria kept the refrigerator full of food and free of black moldy spots; the house smelled vaguely of fresh flowers. Maria had no idea of what to do next, but with an aunt and uncle who cared for her (like her dead-beat mother never did) and far from L.A., this was the best place for her to be right now. She could be helped here.

The next day, after a sleep that had been wanting to happen for days, she felt refreshed. She reached down into her purse to pull out her morning cigarette and felt around. "Damn it. All out," she thought as she pulled out the empty pack. The only tobacco left to her was that little bit of tobacco gut that rattles around the bottom of a pack.

She didn't put on anything beyond the boy shorts and tank top she was wearing, as she grabbed her purse and sandals to go to the corner store. It wasn't that far, just a few houses down, but they didn't have her brand. She walked to the gas station down the street to get her Turkish Silvers, and it felt good to not be walking around the hood. Maria knew you couldn't have nice things in the hood, because people were always trying to take it. Maria knew you couldn't feel good about yourself there, because people are always trying to take that, too.

She smoked a cigarette on the way back, and it was such a good breakfast, that she stopped on the porch to finish a second before she went back into the pretty brick house. Putting the hot cherry out on the sole of her sandal, she flicked the butt into a bare flower pot and opened the door to go back into the cool air conditioning.

And then she saw her aunt and uncle on the floor, bent over on their elbows and knees. They had been taken out, execution-style. The warm blood was pooling underneath them. There was a sting of gunpowder in the room that thirty minutes ago was the most welcoming living room she had ever been in. They know she's here; they might even still be in the house.

She couldn't stay here. Her aunt and uncle were the only people she knew in Phoenix. So she ran. And she left dead, sweet, gentle bodies that wouldn't hurt anybody in her wake.

This Greyhound ride was even more bleak than the last. She wasn't just leaving behind her Gabriela: this time she was leaving behind the only family left that would talk to her. The three dead were the only members of her family she'd even want to talk to: the rest were still in L.A. and were just as low-down as she was. The ticket she bought was as far from anything and anybody she knew as she could afford, without selling off her loot.

A little part of Maria wished she could have been killed instead of those she cared for. Her daily struggle to get by, to eat, to keep clothes on herself, and to not vomit every time she

56

looked at her whore's face in the mirror, it was wearing on her soul. Some people doubt that we have souls. They'd think differently if they met somebody who had lost theirs. Hers was slipping away, and it felt alright, after all the pain she'd caused.

Maria got off the bus in the rundown bus station in downtown Memphis, even though her ticket bought her way to Richmond. As she walked through the trashed, low building, she stepped onto Union Avenue. In the fading light of the summer sun, she didn't pay any mind to the crowd of people gathered on the sidewalks for the baseball game at the towering, red-brick stadium across the street. There was ice in her heart, and no amount of life in any city would thaw that ache.

Memphis would be safe, for a while at least: people that live in L.A. only know about New York, Miami, and San Francisco, so there was no way they would think to look in this hick town in the middle of nowhere. She couldn't actually go to Richmond, because it was an actual city and too close to DC. She needed a place to stay, and even though it looked rundown enough, she knew better than to stay at the dive motel right next to the bus station. If somebody was to come looking for her, that would be a little obvious.

She looked around, looking for another option. There were two up-scale hotels she could see from here. The problem with that kind of place is that they ask questions and want to see some ID, which ain't a problem for people who don't care if they're found. Maria ain't that kind of person.

"You lookin' for somethin', young lady?" croaked the wrinkled, sweaty old black guy sitting on the sidewalk. He was nibbling on some chips from a bag resting on the stained white undershirt covering his slim belly.

Maria decided that he looked dirty enough to be useful. Leaning over to look him in the eyes (and not coincidentally to let her luscious melons dangle like a prize in his face), she said, "Hey, you know a quiet place we can go have a good time?"

The crack-head shook his head "no", protesting, "Go on now. I ain't got no money."

"But honey, you remind me of my daddy. I liked my daddy," she said with lascivious interest.

He heard the hint loud and clear, and his blood-shot eyes lit up his greasy face. His face erupted in a sea of wrinkles as he hooted in filthy triumph. "COME ON!"

The couple walked a few streets south, until the crowds of presentable people disappeared. The whispy black man ducked between two disheveled brick buildings and said, "Come on! Let's get wif tha happy!" as he started to undo his pants.

Maria rolled her eyes. Maybe he was too far gone to be any use after all. In the attempt to salvage this worthless piece of humanity, she countered, "But daddy, this only works if there's a door you can close. I'm gonna scream so loud, I don't want the cops to catch us."

The hobo stopped in mid-unzip, thinking. He looked her over. Tasty caramel thighs. Full breasts. A bangin' ass that looks like it's about to rip its way out of that skirt. Maybe this would be worth owing the guy at the motel $15.

A tedious bus ride down Lamar Avenue later, past the blocks of shuttered retail strips and boarded up houses, the crack-head started pointing excitedly down the way.

"That's yo' ticket to paradise, sweet thang! HEEEEEEE!" he trailed off. The bus continued trundling along, pulling up to its stop before he enticed Maria further by saying, "You been a dirty girl, and daddy's gonna spank you plenty."

She smiled back at him, her thick lips glistening in the fluorescent light of the city bus. She knew there was no way in

Hell she was going to let this piece of shit touch her. "Don't think so, daddy. Try this," she said, slipping her hand into his.

He got confused on the cusp of angry, until he looked down at the thing she left in his paw. A white, jagged rock. Crack. His day was made.

As he shook and hooted in excitement to the mild annoyance of the three other people on the bus, he didn't even notice when Maria's sexy, thick legs walked her tight ass down the steps of the bus and towards the roach motel he brought her to. That night, he'd even forget who he was, when the high overtook him.

From the street, the hotel looked like it was abandoned, but the fact of the matter is that for $15 per day, you can live like a roach king, and nobody who works there will ever recognize you when shown a picture by an investigator. (Editor's note: the name of the hotel will not be revealed, because I couldn't sleep at night if any of you thought it sounded like a good place to stay.)

Maria closed the hollow door and set the chain. She dropped her purse to the worn, green shag carpet. The small, dark-veined mirror over the moldy sink reflected the lone woman illuminated by the desk lamp sitting on the floor. The image of the woman got bigger as she came closer. She was about to wash the grime of days on the Greyhound from her in the basin (there being no shower), but thought better of it. You would have, too: the groan and creak the pipes made when she turned the knob just brought spits of brown, grainy fluid into the bio-hazard of discoloration adorning the sink.

"Great, just great," she thought to herself. Maria was disgusted by this place, and she had done plenty of disgusting things in her life, so she had an abundant frame of reference. A shameful amount of reference. The kind of shame that pokes its head out of the dark corner in your heart and starts gnawing into every feeling inside there.

People like Maria learn how to choke that down and cut it off before they kill themselves. So they numb themselves from the inside out, trying not to feel the feelings that walk hand in hand with sin. Crack distracts the dregs of the street walkers; cocaine is the province of the higher class fuck dolls; crystal meth helps strippers get by. Maria was old-fashioned: she liked the weed. Laced with a bit of angel dust, so maybe she's not that old-fashioned. One hit into that shit, though, and she wouldn't care what the hell anybody thought about her.

She hoped she'd be able to not care, too. She didn't care about the old crack-head she tricked into taking her here: he was fucked to begin with. She had to numb up her brain before the guilt of leaving her aunt and uncle swam back up her river of memory. Hell, who am I kidding: they never left her mind's eye. There they lay on the linoleum, a pool of blood co-mingling their once vital essences, joining them together in death like their love did in life. They had shown her kindness, and what did life pay them back with: death.

The last thoughts that must have swirled in their troubled minds, the terror they felt, the begging, the pleading they must have tried to sway their unnamed killers. "Well," she thought, desperately grasping for anything good, "on the bright side, at least they weren't raped or tortured first." Gabriela didn't have time to be terrified, Maria hoped. Maria only remembered hearing one gun scream, one shot, and then nothing from the woman who gave her shelter. At least hers was quick.

As the drugs and the guilt and the fear fermented in her head, not once did Maria feel bad for what happened to Enrico. He had been a douche-bag before he got popped. Frankly, once she had time to think over what happened, he had been such a cock-bag, she was kind of alright with what happened to him.

Maria dwelt there for a week before she decided to make her move. Maria stepped down from the platform inside the growling bus onto the sidewalk in front of 201 Poplar, the heart of the Memphis criminal "justice" system. If she was going to find anyone to tell about the horrors she witnessed and get revenge for those she left behind, this was her best shot, she thought. If only she had known better.

The building sure didn't look that impressive: yeah, it was big, but it just looked like a bunch of mismatched brick boxes carelessly thrown in a pile. When she made it past the metal detector, she was even mildly disgusted by what she saw: the multi-storied interior looked like the ugliest 1970s shopping mall ever conceived. The wildly distasteful use of colors offended this whore, who was used to the daring and sometimes well thought-out architecture of California.

After inquiring where she might report the litany of dead people somebody was leaving in her wake (well, she left that last bit out) and being helpfully misdirected to the wrong place three or four times, Maria Conchita Sanchez came face to face with the bane of government offices everywhere: an apathetic, fat black woman to talk to.

Maria's blood was pumping, and her stomach fluttered so much she thought she'd pass out. She had plenty of experience trying to hide things from the police, not so much confessing things to them. But that was before someone wanted her dead. She pressed both sweaty palms against the faux-wood countertop and inhaled deeply to steady herself.

This deep, rending, inner personal struggle did not impress or interest the woman at the desk in the slightest. "May I hep you?" she asked, almost in a personal attack.

"I, uh, can I, um."

"Out with it, sweetie."

61

"I need to report a crime."

"Fill this out," the clerk said, tossing a scratched-up clip board onto the counter. There were some forms on it. Maria grabbed the dull No. 2 pencil from the jar on the counter and sat down to fill out the forms. She had expected something more dramatic to be happening right now. Instead, she was just filling out paperwork like she was applying for a job. The fluorescent light overhead flickered a moment, emphasizing the dull, white glare in the room.

Maria finished detailing what had happened and went to hand the form back in.

As the clerk took the clipboard, she said, "Thank you," with a note of finality.

Maria nodded and waited. She watched the woman put the form in a basket, and then go back to filling out a crossword puzzle.

"Excuse me," said Maria.

The black woman looked up at her.

"Can I talk to someone now?"

"If the department finds anything needing investigation, we will contact you within 7-10 business days."

"What?"

"Do you es-peak Engles? That's all we need from you. Have a good day."

"Listen, my whole family is DEAD! I need help, RIGHT NOW! I want to talk to someone NOW!"

The clerk rolled her eyes, "Listen, missy, WE WILL CALL YOU IF WE NEED TO. Now go before I call la migr-"

"Okay, hold on, you two," came a deep, masculine voice. A beast of a blonde police officer stepped from behind Maria to the counter.

"What's the problem here, Gladys?" the officer asked the irate clerk.

"Officer Bachs, this woman is causing a ruckus. She done filled out the form!"

"Alright, thanks, Gladys." Turning his focus to Maria, Officer Bachs said, "Why don't you tell me what your concern is, ma'am, and we'll see what we can do for you, okay?"

Maria shook her head "yes" vigorously, clenching her mouth shut in frustration.

Walking away from the front desk, the man-mountain of a police officer took her statement from the basket and began to review it, asking Maria questions to help flesh out the situation at hand. When Maria looked as though she was going to lose herself in tears, the officer knew the right tactics to keep her engaged in the here and now.

The blonde behemoth nodded his head after the fifteen minute interview, thinking over what she had told him. "Ma'am, since this is an interstate situation, there's another officer I need to bring in on this. Do you mind waiting here for a minute?"

She agreed. Ten minutes later, Officer Bachs returned, with the promised help in tow. The new guy certainly didn't cut the profile of Officer Bachs: he was short, squat, toad-like, black with a speckle of moles, and a thin mustache. He didn't have to be impressive: if he could help, that's all Maria could ask for.

"Hey, so you're Maria Conchita Sanchez? You're the one who filed the report, about California and Arizona?" he asked in a hushed tone.

Maria nodded.

"Aight, come along with me. Officer Bachs, I got it," the chubby man said, as he stepped off to lead Maria away. "This is a special case, and we're moving you to a more secure facility, for your protection."

He moved her along down some corridors, with her only thought being to hold back the tears that wanted to come out. Unlike a lot of Latinas, Maria preferred to keep her business under control in public. He said his real office was in another building, and so he drove her further into downtown, past the towering buildings that were built toward the sky when Memphis was trying to make something of itself.

As he parked in the garage adjacent to city hall, an escort of two black, well-dressed gentlemen walked to the car, opening the doors for both Maria and her driver. They got out of the car and walked in silence towards the building. It didn't escape Maria that she was surrounded by this man and his assistants, and her hackles began to rise. Her host didn't say another word, and she didn't know how much she wanted to ask right now. It was getting dark now, and the shadows of the sun setting beyond the river were falling across the city.

"My, my, my," thundered the cagey baritone of the very tall, very old, white-headed black man that walked into the office whence Maria had been led. He bounced on the balls of his feet, as he stalked into the room on the second floor of city hall. He had a sly look about him, and a physique that bespoke one who enjoyed using his fists with great force, even in old age. Maria went to stand up from her chair in front of the great wooden desk in the mayor's office, but the man motioned for her to sit the fuck down.

He lingered in that commanding stance for a moment, letting his final order set the mood for his unexpected meeting with this delectable and oh-so-in-trouble piece of ass. He was smiling his toothy, white smile at Maria, but she felt danger fill the room just before the man who brought her here opened the door for him. It wasn't hard to tell he was pleased as punch. For Maria, it was harder to tell why.

He spoke first. "Well, well, how you doing, honey?" he asked, his gaze drifting from the unpolished nails on her feet, up her legs, to her bulging bosom, and those sweet, naturally dusted mocha lips. "Mm, mm, mm. So you already saw the name on the desk, so we can cut with the introductions."

While Maria had been scared and numb on the trip to the lair in which she found herself, she had not been so oblivious as to miss that she was in the mayor of Memphis' office. The name on the desk display was one that had long been cursed and blessed by the people of Memphis: "Duke Willie" had been written there for almost twenty years. In a city as violent and deadly as Memphis, many people had been born, lived, and died under the reign of this man. If he had his way, there would be generations more like that.

Maria's mouth moved to speak, but Duke Willie placed a finger from his hand that was big enough to palm a watermelon over his lips to shush her.

"The man isn't done talking yet, girl. Wait your turn," he said, walking to the edge of the desk. He took a seat on one cheek, one leg still standing on the immaculately-kept carpet.

He locked eyes with her, a somber tone in his voice. "You've come a long way, baby. My boy Devon tells me you've been in some shit all across the country. Do you know why?"

Maria's lips moved on their own, like they could answer the question by themselves. Nothing came out. She stopped and looked down. She clenched her eyes shut. Sometimes the simplest answers really are the best ones.

"I fucked with the wrong nigga," she quietly said.

Duke Willie roared in laughing approval of her answer. His chest heaved with the surprise mirth he found at those words, but he managed to start calming down, nodding his head in agreement. "Ho, girl, I guess you right about that! Ho," he trailed off, dabbing at the corners of his eyes to catch the miniscule tears. "Man, girl, you don't even know what you done did, do you? You thought you could jack some ice from some dumb nigga and that would be that!"

Maria's eyes shot up from the floor. She hadn't mentioned anything about the bling she had jacked from Jatarius' room in the police report. She hadn't even mentioned Jatarius. She had only talked about the murders, and, let's face it, she knew there were plenty of people she had burned enough to make them want to fuck her up. How did he know about that?

"Well, since you know why you're here, you deserve to know that I got to give you what's coming to you. See, you fucked with my boys, and you finally got sloppy. Seriously, conyo, of all the places you try to get help, you come to the PD in MY city?! You don't know shit, do you?"

Maria stared at him blankly. What the hell was he talking about?

Duke Willie eased his full-toothed smile. "Tell you what: as a favor to you before I turn you over for the nastiness to come, let me slip into something a little more comfortable. I'll let you go out on top. It'd be a shame for a fine piece like yourself to not go out feeling like a woman for one last time," he said, winking at her.

Her stomach turned, in what she only hoped was the beginning of a massive and lethal internal hemorrhage.

Duke Willie stood to go to the private facilities in his office and "get more comfortable", and then paused, looking at Maria's beautiful face. "You know you could be a New York runway model?"

So, to summarize what just happened: 1) Maria apparently walked into the hands of people who want to do horrible things to her for ripping off that punk-trick Jatarius; 2) they are probably going to torture and kill her; 3) she's about to have less than consensual sex with this filthy old crook as her last hurrah before she dies. Fantastic.

The door to the mayor's private quarters closed shut. A thick breeze from outside wafted through the white curtains in the room. Maria was alone. She cried. Sitting here, she knew she had placed the noose around her own neck. She had caused the death of those near her, and now she was going to join them. All for some fucking money.

As a whore, Maria was pretty numb inside as it was, just to survive. Having a heart was too much to bear in how she lived. She wiped away some snot, and tried to stifle her crying. She doubted Duke Willie was going to be a delicate lover, but fuck that asshole: she wasn't going to let him get off on seeing her crying and begging for mercy. It was time to shut it all down inside. If she already felt dead, it wouldn't really matter when it came.

The dulled sound of Duke Willie singing "do-ba-de-do" could be heard through the door.

She stood up from the place she had been ordered to sit. Standing up straight makes it easier to be defiant. She walked to the window. The curtains parted in the breeze, revealing the cloak of night that had fallen on the world outside. She saw the prison bar-like façade that wrapped all around the upper floors of city hall, and she saw the quiet plaza beyond it.

Looking down, she saw the river-rock concrete ground. There was nothing in her way, nothing holding her in this room with the Duke.

She jumped. Damn the fall.

While she had never been good at gymnastics, she aimed for a head-first landing. Bracing for death, she felt a hard jolt impact her, shocking her so much she couldn't even yell out for the pain it caused. The world went black.

God damn it. She wasn't dead.

Unsure of how long she'd been out, she could tell that she was being carried, her arms on the shoulders of two men. They were wearing polo shirts and khakis. "Fuck it, they got me. Game over," she resigned herself.

One of the men took notice of her waking, whispering, "We're friends."

"Where are you taking me?" she quietly croaked.

"We're getting you away from that den of thieves. Care to join us for a drink?"

It seemed odd that kidnappers would politely ask her to come along for a drink. Fuck it. Whatever.

Maria didn't bother raising her head to look where she was being taken. If she had, and craned her neck back far enough to take it all in, she would see a Gothic tower, lording over the city in magnificent abandonment. The yellow, aged walls stood accented with gold, but only darkness could be found within its hundreds of windows. Once the tallest building in the South, a temple erected to capitalism, it stood hollow on its consecrated ground.

Slipping through the boards put in place to keep hoodlums and hobos out, she heard a groan of metal and was carried into the darkness. A few steps in, however, the darkness was not the pitch blackness she thought it would be: from within the heart of the building came a pale, bone white light. Breathing in the musty air, she looked around her, hearing only quiet and the clacking of the heels of her bearers' dress shoes.

She beheld the lost grandeur of the Moorish hall and its limestone and granite bones. The deep color of the walls evoked to her the tomb of a long-slumbering king, waiting for the stars to be right for his return. As they walked further in, she began to hear the thumping of bass, and the light grew brighter. Glancing over her shoulder, she saw the darkened trail that brought her here looked brighter than when she had first stepped foot on it.

She whispered a question to her bearers, as though she would disturb something beyond the reach of light. "Where am I?"

"You've been invited to Parliament. You can never let anyone know that," was all that would ever be said to her about that.

Maria asked her escort, "Where are you taking me?"

She was curtly answered, "To meet some friends."

The trio stopped at a pair of black doors through which pierced the scintillating ray of white light that guided them here. One of her companions released her and stepped to one side of the door to gain them entrance, in some manner arcane. The other held onto her arm even after she had steadied herself. She was his charge, and he would not risk her flight.

The doors opened inward, revealing a swirling vortex of pulsing lights, thumping bass, and smoke. The hall was not ablaze with fire (not entirely, anyway, for there were braziers suspended from on high holding dancing flames), but the fog meant to keep revelers cool in the depths of their orgiastic dancing. She saw before her a multi-tiered hall filled with dancers and revelers, glowing lights flashing through the crowd, and above it all a steady hand at the mixing board, conducting the ebbs and flows of the epic rave consuming all those in its grasp.

Even from the edge of the chaos, this event horizon that both robbed and created memories, Maria felt the bass rolling through her like an unstoppable spirit, the force of it shaking her very core. There's no telling how many hours the revelers, comprised of every shade and hue of the rainbow, had been swaying in this sea of bodies, passion, and energy.

Her hosts moved swiftly to the heart of the chaos, pulling her through the gates just before they clacked shut. The heavy sound of their closing was the sound of a boom dropping, but even that roar went almost unnoticeable in the din of light and life. The bodies of those enraptured slid off her escorts like oil and water, but she found herself catching on those she passed by. The smell of bodies and heat and perfumes and lust was palpable in a way of which she was well familiar. The eyes, the fingers of those engulfing her and her boatmen touched her, grazed her, sought her. These were welcome eyes, eyes that wanted everything she was willing and wanting to give them, and nothing that she wanted to keep for herself.

What had she kept for herself?

She felt the firm hands of her guides on her, but she felt so many more. It became hard to tell whither she was to go, with whom, or where she was. In the heart of the chamber, she looked up to see a setting sun looking warmly down upon her from afar off, and she felt the full force of the thundering bass that wanted to change who she was. She didn't know if she would mind that kind of salvation.

However, those hands that delivered her into this paradise brought her past the siren's rocks. She was finally wrenched from the grip of the hedonism into a golden elevator. The door shut, accompanied by a "ding" that sounded suspiciously like James Brown saying, "Get down!"

There were no floor numbers that lit up as they ascended, but Maria knew they had to be moving fast enough to cover such ground. This was an elevator for those who knew the way to where they wanted to go, not those who needed to be told when to get off. The leering Olmec heads worked into the gold would not make the choice for you.

One of the men in the pin-stripe suits pressed a button set into the eye of a golden sun, bringing the elevator to an immediate, smooth halt, accompanied by the elevator emitting a raspy, black tone hollering, "HEY!"

The doors slid open to show a drab concrete hallway, strips of black light running the length of the walkway to another door. The trio walked purposefully down the hall, but Maria's interest was piqued along the way. She saw tiny, isolated openings in the ceiling, and recessed circles lining both high and low points along the walls. This wasn't just a hallway: this was a death trap.

But not today. One of the men leaned over to a featureless side of the door frame and made entrance for the group, the other man pushing the way open. Maria was quickly brought into a slick VIP room, lit by neon lights decorating the ceiling and walls. There was already a party going on up here, with almost a dozen people in play.

Her eyes were instantly drawn to the two men in command of the situation. With a woman on each arm and leg, a large, older gentleman decked out in a sleek-cut suit smirked at his younger partner, a dark-headed man in the process of exhaling a plume of smoke as tall as a Grizzlies forward. Maria had seen people hit a bong like that before, which meant this man was a professional. They laughed with good cheer afterwards, before returning to the business at hand.

The men that brought her to the room held her in place just inside the chamber, as it wasn't her turn for an audience yet. She could see that the man currently in the hot seat wasn't having a good time.

"So, I'll say this again. Do you know what you're here for?" asked the dark-haired younger man. He was slightly tan with slicked-back hair, with the sparkle in his keen eyes matched against his shockingly white suit. When he started rocking side to side in his high-backed executive chair, Maria noticed the nickel-plated revolver in his right hand. He was lazily swaying it around to add the right tone to the interview.

One of Maria's escorts quietly grumbled in her ear, "You're going to answer some questions, when it's your turn. The one with the gun you will call Princess. The one with the women you will call Spectre. Make no sudden moves."

Maria couldn't help but whisper without looking back, "Why is he called Princess?"

"It's a cover name. Don't ask," was all her handler advised.

Kneeling on the polished hardwood floor before Princess was a bruised young man with dirty blonde hair, his hands zip-tied behind his back. His thin, fair beard was streaked with blood. "Am I getting lectured by a drug kingpin for breaking the law?" he asked incredulously.

Princess jumped up, fury rising in his baritone voice. "YES, DOUGLAS, YOU ARE! You listen to me, you little punk. There is a difference between what is acceptable and what is unacceptable."

"Asshole, I made you a fat stack, so you better cut this bullshit before I-"

WHACK. The blonde hipster lay on the ground, brought low by a back-hand by the man in white. Princess pointed his index finger in judgment at the blonde man on the floor, saying, "Listen, you little shit: we don't sell to kids. We don't trade goods to kids for sex. We don't give the goods to kids to watch them have sex."

"Dude, they were 17, and they were hot as hell, you faggot," the blonde youth proclaimed in exasperation, trying to defend his licentiousness.

WHOOM. The blonde man gasped in pain, as the air in his chest was kicked out of him. A few swings of his black

72

dress shoes later, Princess composed himself. Smoothing back his unruffled hair, he continued his tirade.

"See, Douglas, that's what makes us different. We sell to people who can handle their shit. We sell to grown-ups. We sell to people who don't freak out when their idiot friend, who can't handle their shit, O-Ds and call the cops! They were 17 this time, but what about next time?" he asked rhetorically. Motioning to the two men standing stoically behind Douglas, Princess quietly ordered, "Get him out of here."

As the two bent over to pick up the convicted, the black man of the pair asked, "Where do you want him?"

Thinking it over for a moment, Princess finally decided. "Fuck him. Send him to Guatemala." He turned his away as the two men took the garbage out, walking to a gleaming sink against the back wall. He poured some water out to wash the filth off his hands, and splashed it on his face to freshen his senses.

Spectre looked up from the women on his arms to notice Maria, as if she had just appeared. The older man in sleek black silk said matter-of-factly to his partner, "We've got company."

Princess finished toweling the water from his brow before he looked over his shoulder to see Maria. Throwing the towel down, he yelled at the rest of the women, "Get out, you hussies! Men got business!" The bevy of buxom beauties knew better than to protest and just left, blowing kisses at the relaxed Spectre as they went out the door. Maria's escorts stepped out with them.

The older man stood to speak, cordially asking Maria, "May we get you anything? An aperitif? A distraction?" he suggested, his hand sweeping toward a tray of pills and pre-cut lines of white.

"I'm fine," was all she said, unsure if she would ever eat of those fruits again.

73

Princess nodded along as Spectre went through the formalities, but once concluded he yelled at Maria in a full-throated blast, "What the fuck are you so wanted for?!"

"I don't know," she said, the weariness evident in her voice.

"What were you doing with the mayor then?"

"He was going to fuck me." No surprise in her tone, no sense of threat.

"If Duke Willie wanted to fuck you, he'd have put you in prison and softened you up first, so you'd be nice and pliable when he got you out. He never has anybody brought straight to him."

"Why did your men pick me up?"

The younger man pinched the bridge of his nose. Focus on your breathing. Don't be so tense, he thought to himself. In a calm tone, he replied, "Because Willie wanted you so bad. We had to find out why. That's why." He paced around the room. "And you were helpful enough to jump out a window, so our guys who caught wind of you at the police station were in just the right place to snatch you off the pavement and get you out of there. Now why did he want you so bad?"

She honestly didn't know what to tell him. The only clues she had were from Duke Willie's gloating, so that's where she started the tale. She recounted everything, from the moment she stalked toward her prey, Jatarius, to the party at John's mansion built on sin. She cleared him out of all the ice in the room, and slipped out. Then the death. All the death.

She finished her story, standing where Douglas had just been brought to judgment. Spectre and Princess sat back in their executive chairs, taking it all in, thinking through the angles. Attention to detail is what got them where they were, and it was what kept them ahead of their enemies. And alive.

Spectre's mustachioed lips framed the question, "Is that all?"

"Yes. That's all I know," said Maria, her voice starting to choke. She didn't know why all this happened, and she felt like she kept coming up short in trying to figure it out.

Princess pressed the point. "So you're telling us that you ripped off a hood-rat that sold some weed to a porn kingpin, and not only did they have the resources, intel, and drive to find and try to kill you, they followed you to a place they couldn't have known you'd go and tried it again, only to then follow you to Phoenix and kill your family for it? And over a thousand miles away, Duke Willie knew about what you did, which you don't even know, and he's in with them to the point of capturing and handing you over for whatever they're going to do to you. For stealing some jewelry. From a hood-rat. I ain't buying it."

"Who else did you screw over?" asked Spectre.

"This is it! This is all I got," she shrieked, upending the contents of her purse onto the nearest table. The bling cascaded out, dazzling in the neon lights like a purple rain. Maria had to shake the purse several times to dislodge the most stubborn pieces of loot. For good measure, she took off the pieces she was wearing and threw it onto the pile.

"Wow. I'd be pissed, too," said Princess, in shock at the mound of high priced jewelry she just dumped out of her Gucci knock-off.

Eye-balling the pile of lucre, Spectre reached over to it, running his fingers through the goods. His hand stopped suddenly, his fingers grasped, and he pulled a thumb drive out of the pile of wadded Benjamins and chains.

Princess' eyebrows rose in interest, and he smacked his lips. "Well. Let's see what we have here," he said, snatching the thumb drive from the older man's outstretched palm. He stalked across the room to a laptop sitting open atop the rich mahogany desk at the back of the room and plugged it in. A few moments of silent clicking later, he laughed out loud, stomping his heels in amazement.

"Spectre! I know why she's such a wanted piece of ass! There's an entire network of narco-terrorist, al-Qaeda bullshit here! This is enough shit to indict some of the biggest businessmen and politicians in the country. In the world! Now that makes sense! Who the hell leaves this in a nightstand?" he finished, puzzled.

Maria was speechless. She had no clue that's what she had. Her shock turned to panic: when the initial surprise cooled down, she remembered that her hosts were drug pushers themselves. Maybe there was dirt on them they'd rather keep quiet on that thumb drive.

She asked plainly and without fear, "What are you going to do with me?"

Spectre looked her over, with the kind of calculation in his eyes she expected to see in John's eyes. In an even tone of voice, he told her, "Go with the men that brought you here. They have a room you can stay in."

"I don't want to go. I'm tired of moving and never stopping."

"Maria, you're safe here. You are among friends. You have nothing to fear from us," he continued, as he stood up to step closer to her. "See, we're the chivalrous types."

Princess chimed in with agreement, "Chivalry ain't dead," as he continued flipping through the files. "And besides, we invited you in. We'd at least wait for you to leave before we'd kill you."

The older man finished, "Unless you try to cross us, we've got no beef with you. You need some rest."

76

Maria nodded silently and turned around, walking measured steps toward the door. She went with the two armed men waiting outside, fully aware that she was trapped here. As Princess' display of indulged violence on one of his own people demonstrated, they would do with her what they wanted.

The VIP room was cleared out, and the two friends found themselves alone in the room, quiet except for the dull thumping of the bass below. The air grew very close in light of the smoke and the revelation. Such a small place was not fit to discuss big ideas.

"Let's get some fresh air," said Spectre.

Princess grabbed the thumb drive and shoved it in his pocket. The two exited the room, down the strafing chamber and into the elevator, to down below the city. Spectre knew where to stop, and the two stepped into an underground tunnel. It looked as though it might have once been a subway terminal, now long forgotten. Indeed, these two men were the only people still alive that even knew it was here.

The two men walked in silence to where the tunnel ended at a railed, open-aired platform overlooking the Mississippi River. Spectre leaned on both hands, staring out over the waters rippling in the night's light. "This is big news. Real big news," started Spectre.

Princess nodded. "Just from first glance, there's enough in there for us to find all the connections between some of the dirtiest players in the game. All over the world, and right here at home. We're gonna know where all the joints to break are to destroy some heinous people."

"Is Duke Willie in there?" Spectre asked, not looking away from the waters.

"His was the first name I searched for."

"What do we got on him?"

"Names of suppliers, money launderers, insurers, dealers, allies, dirt he's got on people to keep them pliable. The works."

"Anybody we can take?"

"Of course we can take them. We're bad asses," replied Princess, mildly insulted over the insinuation.

"I'm serious, my friend. We've got our stuff together, but the fact is Duke Willie is the top dog for four states. We can hold our own, and have, but can we take down the king? Can we keep the other groups in town from launching a war with us if we made a play for supremacy?"

"I think so," said the younger man. "I saw parts we could carve up to make it worth their while. And there's Willie's people we can take out or flip to our side. We won't have to skulk like lesser men beneath the colossus in our hometown anymore."

Money and power were great, but that wasn't what was on Spectre's mind every day. The picture on his nightstand he gazed at lovingly every night didn't have a dollar bill in it. It held the only woman that he had ever really loved, all that he had left of her. His Dorothy. His precious Dorothy that Duke Willie let die. It was never enough for Duke Willie to conquer: he had to desolate and burn, until all under his power had nothing left to fight for. None of this would bring her back.

Princess carried on, oblivious to the inner pain of his old friend. "We can't stop with Willie. There's more we can take down and set to right. There's enough dirt here to bring down some of the biggest pricks and evil masterminds alive and breathing: crooks on Wall Street, senators, police chiefs, cartels, dictators, terrorists. All of these bastards making billions off white slavery, terrorism, and blood dope (like blood diamonds, just snortable - ed.) can go down with all this. We can take down this wall, one brick at a time. We can make the world, this city, a better place."

As his younger compatriot dreamed big, Spectre was not so sure that all that was even possible. "Okay, we may be able to take down Duke Willie, but that won't be easy, and who knows if we'll live through that? For the sake of Memphis, yes, we'll take the gamble, but all the rest? Buddy, we're only two chumps on a stump in a city on a bluff: how are we ever going to take down all those other guys? Would it even make any difference if we did? We can't take all their spots, and who will replace them when they're gone?"

Princess listened to the old man and gestured for Spectre to continue. Spectre sighed, continuing, "My friend, we're not clean ourselves. What makes you think we'd wind up doing any different? Will the blood and the suffering be worth it?"

"We've got our faith. And we're already different. We don't aim to hurt the lives we touch," was the answer.

Spectre still felt a pain in his heart. He wanted to wreck Duke Willie, make him BLEED, and hear him scream for what he had done. The sweet woman he let die, the lives he had ruined, all because Spectre tried to stand up to the man who promised to bring even more racism and violence to this troubled city.

The women Spectre surrounded himself with helped him forget about her sometimes, but they never healed the wound. What if his friend went down in a hail of gunfire in this war he wanted to start? Who would help keep Spectre from going to that dark place and bringing its fury back with him?

Tears began to form in the hefty man's eyes. "Why are we even doing this? I mean, think about what we already have. There's so much evil in the world, how arrogant are we to think we'll make a hill of beans difference? Why are we even here? After everything we've done has cost us, why keep going?" was his final exclamation, as the tears rolled down.

Princess put his arm around the shoulders of his troubled friend. He let him weep. But not forever. Princess finally said, "It's got to be worth it. What else can we do? We're still alive. Would you prefer to sit here and wait for relentless time to run down the clock? You're right, we're not clean, but we're already done so much good with the little empire we've built. The other good guys want to fix the problem from the outside, which will never work so long as this stuff is illegal.

"So we get dirty to take back the night. That's what makes us different. We have been given this knowledge and the ability to do something about it. We would be cowards and lesser men than we are to do nothing."

The two men stood at the edge of the platform, overlooking the Great River, rolling forever on, as it always has, tonight under darkened sky.

In her quiet room, Maria was all alone with her thoughts. Only the double tequila sunrise kept her company. She was really beyond caring at this point. She just wanted it to end. She didn't even feel the fear anymore. She didn't feel anything. Just a dull sense of regret. And tired. So tired.

She sat, staring down, when she heard a knock at her door. She opened it to see a composed, resolute Spectre standing there. Maria opened the door without a word, stepping aside for him to enter.

As the door clicked shut after him, he told her, "What you brought us is an amazing gift that will topple tyrants. What do you want for it?"

"I want my life back."

"I can't give you that."

"I want to go home."

"Your home is gone."

"I want to see my family."

"Someday you will, just not in this lifetime."

"I want to live."

He stepped up to her, locking her eyes to his. "If you want to live, here's what's going to happen: you're going to talk to a nice man named Feng, who will make you a different person; I'm going to touch you up a bit, make their pictures of you not look like you; you're going on a mission trip to a place with a name you'll find out when you get there; they'll never find you again; we'll make them pay. All of them."

She understood.

He walked closer to her, a kind strength in his eyes. He touched her chin, lifting it so that she may drink in the comfort he brought her. "I cannot bring back the dead, but I can avenge them. I cannot set the world to how it was, before the reaper came. I cannot put the petals back on the rose, now that we're fallen. But we can live this life with all that we have left to us. We can't undo the damage, but maybe we can grow past the scars."

The Night of the Ettercap
By Stephen Clements

"I don't care what this 'honorable court' thinks or wants, none of you are ever going to believe me anyway. There is no way in God's green Hell that any of you are going to buy this. I saw it, and it happened, but you're going to have me committed if I tell the jury what I saw out there. I'd rather be charged with contempt."

Father Matthew Dunnigan was a little upset. If you had been through what he had and been told to tell the story exactly as it happened to a courtroom of people who hadn't, you'd know for a fact they'd call you a lunatic, too. Better to leave them guessing.

1982, Church of the Emaculation, Collierville

Yeah, it's a steady job being a priest, but the perks aren't that great: you get to spend your time listening to old people tell you "dirty secrets" about how they used to lust after their neighbor's wife, husband, or horse when they could still get it up, or attend tons of potluck social clubs, where kept housewives tried to do something with their days. Sure, there were some eye-appealing teenage girls that came to service, but they were always covered head-to-toe, and it was against Church law to do anything to get them less dressed. Maybe there were better ways to get a good education in theology than to do it the hard way.

"But," remembered Father Matthew Dunnigan, "at least I'm not in Ohio anymore. Thank the Almighty for that." Even growing up there and not knowing anything else, he knew Ohio had to be a form of punishment from God, but for what sin he didn't know. Let's face it, buck-eyes suck, and it is way too cold all the damn time. To get out of there, he could either join the Army or join the priesthood. Having talked to the couple morons who came home on leave from the Army, the priesthood seemed like a better idea. He was afraid his brains and all the book-learning he had in it would get smashed out by a rifle butt.

Saint Jerome's Seminary in New York was a way out for all that. Far away from that hick town he grew up in, Matt was expected to live by a code of conduct as a student, but he found a way around that, some of the time. One thing he liked about the education he was getting in New York, as opposed to old provincial Ohio, was that it was way more his style: what he learned didn't agree with everything his dad told him. He was being educated, given access to new books, new ideas, old ideas, whole new Hells he had never heard of, and he was getting to see more of the world.

People in his old town lived and died in the same damn town their parents did. Here he was learning in depth about the history of the Church, Jesus' acts and deeds, but it was almost fashionable for his teacher-priests to dismiss the dogma of their own religion. They might preach it as gospel, but with a slight smirk and a wink, just so their flock didn't take it too seriously. It was subversive. He liked it. He was wrong.

But he didn't find out about that last part until much later. Namely, two years after he moved down to Collierville, Tennessee, an old hick suburb of Memphis. This was back in the day before Collierville got colonized by FedEx pilots and their families in pink brick McMansions, back when the town was covered in cow pastures and farms. You might ask why Father Dunnigan would want to ever go near a small hick town again, but he chose this over an assignment to Los Angeles. Call it familiarity breeds content. Or maybe he heard that Memphis was a flashpoint of black culture and couldn't get enough of BB King and Isaac Hayes.

Whatever the reason was, he was sick of Pam and Harold Pickles, the old couple who would not quit inviting him over for dinner tonight after the service. "Listen," he thought to himself, "thanks for the compliments on the service (which I worked on for about fifteen minutes yesterday), but please go home so I can get to the bottle of moonshine waiting in my house."

"Well, thank you, Mrs. Pickles. I am sure your meatloaf is just as delightful as last time you treated me to it, but I have a very sick soul to go be with tonight." That's what he actually said.

The white-haired old woman doddered for a moment, blinking quietly as she took his answer and ran it through the slow processor in her head.

"Okay, Father. Thanks for the service. Come on, dear," Mr. Harold said, thankfully rescuing everyone from the situation at hand.

"Goodbye, Father," said Mrs. Pickles, her Southern drawl in full effect. It was as thick and slow as molasses dripping down the wall.

Father Matthew watched them turn and slowly dodder to their old blue pick-up truck. "God is good," he always said.

"Father Dunnigan? Are you there?"

Damn it. Pam Pickles again. It was 10 o'clock at night; what the hell did she want at this hour? Especially after I've had this much to drink. "Mrs. Pickles, heeello. What can I do for you?" answered Father Dunnigan.

The old lady, having been duly invited, launched into a panic. "FATHER!" the old lady screeched. "I need you to come over here right now! This house is possessed. Come quickly, we need you to save us!"

84

What the bloody Hell? "What's that, Mrs. Pickles? I'm sorry, I didn't hear you correctly. What was that again?" asked the heavily inebriated young priest.

"Mr. Pickles and I were watching the TV, and we saw this show about a ghost that haunts a house. All the stuff he did on the TV happens in this house, WE NEED YOU RIGHT NOW!"

This is why technology is a bad thing: one, it gives stupid people ideas; two, it gives them the ability to get in touch with other people and share their stupid ideas.

"Uh, Mrs. Pickles, please, really, it is very late. It's just a work of fiction. The TV show is not real."

"Oh yes, it was! It had that law enforcement officer from the other shows on there, and it's true with all that's going on."

"Mrs. Pickles, did you just see 'The Ghost and Mr. Chicken' with Don Knotts?"

"Oh yes, Officer Fife was in the show about the ghost possessing the house."

"No, Mrs. Pickles, that was a movie. It didn't really happen. It's not real. Now please, go to bed."

"IT'S REAL, FATHER! I SAW IT MYSELF!"

"Mrs. Pickles, please put Mr. Pickles on the line. I have special instructions for him on how to take care of the ghost in your house."

"OH, OKAY," she helpfully agreed. With a loud CLACK, she put the bulky ear piece down on the table, so she could shuffle away to fetch her husband.

"Wow. Why can an Irishman not have a good drunk in peace?" Matt wondered to himself.

"Hello, Father," came the wavering old voice of Mr. Pickles.

Ah, the reasonable one. "Mr. Pickles, please, your house is not possessed by a ghost. It's just a show, a fictional show, you saw. It was make-believe."

"Really? So then we don't have a ghost in the house? We have heard a lot of strange noises around the house, especially at night," said Mr. Pickles.

"I'm sure it's not possessed or haunted. But I do want you to do something to make sure, okay?" offered the priest.

"Oh, okay," said Mr. Pickles.

"I need the two of you to sit around the kitchen table, hold hands, and pray that God keeps your house pure and insoluble, er, I mean, sacrosanct. Yes, that should do for tonight, and the sun coming up will take care of the rest, okay?"

"Oh, okay, that sounds real good. Thank you, Father."

"Thank you, good night."

"God bless you, Father."

"Yeah, that. Thanks, bye," Matt hang up swiftly.

The small television set on Father Dunnigan's countertop flickered, the antenna doing its best to pick up Channel 5 News at 11. Now that the Pickles' could go screw themselves for the rest of the night, his vision focused a bit when the reporter started talking about a young boy who had gone missing in Memphis. Something about his simpleton mother being brought in by the police for questioning in connection with the young boy's disappearance.

"Sick freak," murmered Matt, as he blearily heard the story unfold. He had seen it happen before up North: mom goes nuts, strangles/drowns/stabs her own flesh and blood until it stops moving, then freaks out and hides the body. Why the fuck did that freak bother having that tender little boy in the first place? She could have given it up for adoption, or just left it at grandma's house and disappeared into the night. It was

Memphis: people do things like that here. There's songs about it.

Father Matthew Dunnigan woke up the next day, his head suddenly splitting with pain, as the glass on his front door was being slapped viciously. He rolled over on the linoleum floor of his kitchen and slowly got off the ground, accompanied by the incessant slapping.

He unlocked the deadbolt and then stopped before unlocking the rest. He ducked over to check himself out in his reflection on the pane of the microwave oven. "Okay, not too bad," he thought.

Opening the door, the harsh fall morning sun blasted him in the eyes. "FATHER DUNNIGAN!" came the crackly, old female voice. Mr. and Mrs. Pickles. At 8:23 in the morning, on his door step.

The excessive noise hit his ears like a brick. "Mrs. Pickles, hello. Good morning. What are you doing here?" asked Father Dunnigan.

"FATHER! The cows were attacked Father! I told you it was an evil ghost in the house! They're eating the cows!" the old lady crowed.

Matthew had to slow her down. "Wait, wait. Mr. Pickles, what's going on?"

"Calm down, dearie, let me talk to the man," cautioned Mr. Pickles, as he patted his wife's shoulder. "Father Dunnigan, we came over because two of the cows have gone missing. The rest of the herd is spooked, and so are we."

This is what his parishioners bothered him for at 8:23 in the morning.

"Well, did you tell the police? Animal control? They could tell you if there are any wolves in the area."

Mr. Pickles held his wife back from raising another ruckus, and the old man adjusted his heavy spectacles before he answered, "This was no coyote attack. There's no sign of a struggle, and the coyotes would have left the bodies near the edge of the woods. And we have coyotes down here, not wolves."

"Whatever it is you have down here, this sounds like something the cops should investigate for you. Maybe call your insurance adjuster," offered Father Dunnigan, hoping they would listen and leave him the heck alone.

This was the last straw for Mrs. Pam Pickles. After ten minutes of verbal bludgeoning and laceration from the startled old woman, Father Dunnigan, in his weakened state, begged for mercy and agreed to come to the house later. With that concession won, the old parishioners tottered off, leaving Father Matthew to recover from the Day of the Lord.

The herd of cattle moaned and mooed, as it pressed up against the fence closest to the house. Out of the acres of pasture open for them to graze on, every last one of them was pushing themselves up against the fence. "That is kind of weird," Father Matthew thought.

As he stood on the back porch in the early twilight, Mr. Pickles came up to him, doing a lot of yammering on about the cows and the lay of the pasture, with the woods at the back of the lot. Basically, the priest realized, he was going to be held hostage with kindness by these old, reliable parishioners until he exorcised the house.

It was ridiculous, the rite of exorcism. All it did was feed into people's superstitions and distract them from real problems in their lives. Does your house make strange noises in the dark of night? Your house is settling. Does your kid act like a brat non-stop and cuss up a storm in church? There's something wrong with the kid's head, and you're probably responsible for it. Blaming demons for all of life's problems is a crappy way of dealing with your issues.

Heck, Father Matthew didn't even know the rite of exorcism, so he just made some stuff up that looked convincing. As a parish priest, he didn't even have the authority to perform the rite of exorcism in the Catholic Church: his bishop would have to appoint someone to do it or do it himself. Matthew was not about to look stupid by asking his superior to come exorcise a cow pasture.

After waving his hands and reading some verses from his Bible at the house, the Pickles insisted he do the whole farm, but he was able to extricate himself from that situation. That bit of sleight of hand was enough to allay the worst of his parishioners' hysterics, and that was good enough for him.

"FATHER DUNNIGAN!" came the old, shrill voice of Pam Pickles on the other end of the phone. It might be time to get a different phone number.

"WHAT?! I mean, yes, Mrs. Pickles, how are you?" replied Father Matthew. He was sober, because he had the feeling this was going to happen. He didn't know yet what "this" was, but he knew it was coming.

"FATHER DUNNIGAN," she hollered into the wrong end of the receiver. There was a weird, strangled, beastly noise in the background. That was creepy. "It's happening again! This time the ghost is killing the cows! Come quickly!"

What? What did she just say? "Wait, what, Mrs. Pickles? The cows are being attacked? Call the police, I'll come over."

When he got to the Pickles' farm, he saw what she had been so frantic about. Wow, she had really understated how awful the sight was.

89

Mr. Pickles led Father Dunnigan through the house, past a hysterical, shotgun- toting Mrs. Pickles, to the back porch they had just been on earlier today. He didn't know if he should throw up or scream and run from what he saw lying there.

The crying herd in the background was just as startled and confused as their owners at the sight and stench of their mutilated brother on the porch. Illuminated by the spotlight on the back of the house, there lay what must have been a cow, charitably described now as a carcass, emaciated, lacerated, oozing green puss, and discolored all over its brown hide with patches of sickly blue, rotten black, and jaundiced yellow. The thing was practically falling apart, with congealed blood and puss all over. When it twitched, Father Dunnigan tripped and fell off the side of the rail-free wooden porch.

Even though his neck was what broke his fall, Father Matthew sprang back to his feet, eyes wide with terror. "WHAT THE HELL IS THAT?!" he shouted.

"That's what the missus called you about, Father," answered Mr. Pickles. "We were sitting there watching the TV, when we heard a loud crash on the back porch. We came out here and ol' Barney here was waiting on us. He went missing a month ago. I wish he had stayed gone if he meant to come back like this."

"AAAUUHH," cried Father Dunnigan. This was the most horrible thing he had ever seen. It would soon be challenged by several others.

"This is why we asked you to bless all the property," Mr. Pickles said.

Father Matthew knew he had to do something. "Give me a flashlight, and let's look around the property. We have to find what did this."

"Okay, let me get the shotgun from the missus," Mr. Pickles said. He shuffled into the house, and came back out toting the shotgun, while Mrs. Pickles made some incoherent shouting from inside.

The two of them made their way into the pen and looked up and down the pasture in the dark of night. The cops never showed, even though Mrs. Pickles called several times. An hour passed, but there was no sign of coyotes. However, there was a patch of the wire fence at the edge of the woods that was torn all to hell.

The two grown men stood there, staring at the gaping hole. It was really dark out, the light shed by the spotlight on the porch a distant beacon bringing no comforting light this far out. The pathetic flashlights they held did not reassure them that it was a good idea to keep going into the night-shrouded woods. Being sensible men, they agreed to go back to the house and keep an eye on the herd from edge of the pen. Sure, they could have sat on the rocking chairs on the porch, but they had no wish to go anywhere near the porch.

The next day, the Pickles agreed to stay put and keep an eye on the herd. Much more importantly, they decided to do something with that desiccated carcass on the back porch. Father Matthew, still jumpy from the adrenaline that rushed into his system last night, drove to the police station to see why the heck they never showed up, despite several pledges to do just that. That was a wasted trip.

Even with the parish priest personally pleading for somebody, anybody, to come out and take a look at the thing that got left on the porch. The cops didn't care. "It was just a coyote," they said, not looking up from the newspaper, "happens all the time."

"There is no way that coyotes did this," protested the priest. Father Matthew gave a detailed description of the fetid corpse that something threw onto the five-foot tall porch.

"Probably some kid's prank," the cop answered.

"Are you serious?! A group of kids tortured and mangled this cow, then, without a truck or any equipment, threw the rotten cow's body onto an elevated platform?!"

"Listen," said the bored police officer at the desk, "we've got our hands full helping look for this little kid whose mom killed him. We've got a lot of searching to do, and a dead cow just ain't that important."

"Well, two other cows have gone missing, too. Can one of you just come out and look to see if there are any clues about what happened to them?" asked the priest.

He might as well have gone for a walk in the park: these cops were damn useless.

Since the town library was not that far of a walk, Father Matthew decided to go look in there. Research was something he was always good at in school, and maybe there was something in the library's newspaper archives about this. This was clearly not a coyote attack, and no punk kids did this. Flipping through the bound volumes of The Commercial Appeal and the Memphis Press-Scimitar, he found a lot of old Elvis pictures and some stuff on E.H. Crump, but when it came to deranged atrocities involving cattle, the coverage was a little thin.

He found a few small articles about coyote attacks in the periphery of Shelby County and some kids' pranks involving police scolding teenagers caught tipping cows. There was one incident, in Fisherville, just up the road from here, that looked like it would be promising. That turned out to be a bust, though, as most of the article consisted of quotes from the spooked hick farmers, and one line about the "grisly remains" of the cow. No pictures. Not a thing to go on.

Driving his blue Cutlass Supreme back to the Pickles' farm, Father Dunnigan decided the only way to get to the bottom of this was to go look in the woods for himself. The cops weren't going to do anything, so it fell to him to look after his flock. He did happen to pick up a crucifix and dip several vials of holy water, just to comfort the Pickles, of course. For their sake.

"What did you find out, Father?" asked the weary Mr. Pickles, as Father Dunnigan closed his heavy car door.

The young priest walked up to the back porch, his eyes searching for the hideous bovine corpse on the wooden planks. Thank God: they moved the body. He didn't ask what they did with it.

"Not much," he answered, squinting in the late afternoon sun. "The police are tied up right now with searching for that unfortunate child from the news. They don't have any officers to provide. It's left to us to settle this."

The wrinkled, old man nodded, his drooping chin shaking as he did so. "The missus has taken a rest inside. Would you care to do the same? I reckon we need to be rested up to keep an eye out tonight."

"Mr. Harold, you should go ahead and get some sleep. I'm going to go looking in the woods while we still have some sunlight, but I'll take you up on the offer when I get back. I will take some coffee, if you have any ready."

Mr. Pickles did have just that, and after giving out a heady shot of caffeine-laced liquid, the old man bedded down. Father Dunnigan politely declined the offer to carry the shotgun with him, but did take a flashlight, at Mr. Pickles' insistence. "Those woods go deep," he said.

Trekking past the uneasy herd, Father Dunnigan walked across the open, green field. His eyes hurt from lack of sleep, and he ached all over. His neck was really sore, but he knew he couldn't sleep right now. If he lay still long enough, he knew he'd wake up too stiff to move, much less find out what the hell did that to the poor cow.

He saw the ruined barbed fence at the edge of the pasture, and it looked even less appealing with the light of day on it. The wires had not been cleanly clipped, like with bolt cutters. The metal stake that tied the fence together was also broken off at the base, which was completely unnecessary: an intruder would just have to cut the wires to get through; there was no need to break the stake. How did the stake get broken to begin with?

He crossed himself and splashed a few drops of holy water on the breach. He wasn't sure what good it would do, but it felt good to do something. But what did this?

Father Matthew stalked through the forest, trying to be quiet, even as his loafers crunched on the piles of fallen leaves that carpeted the woods. There were plenty of fresh leaves on the ground now, with the trees half denuded of their foliage in the face of encroaching winter. He hopped across small streams and dead logs, ducked one low-lying branch only to be poked in the eye by the sharp twigs sticking out just behind it. Fortunately, it had been pretty dry out, as dry as it ever was in the Mississippi Valley.

Twilight was creeping up, and Father Matthew was about to turn back when his eyes caught something: the bank of leaves on the opposite side of a tiny stream looked like something really large had been dragged through it. This far in the woods, there was no way a truck or even 4-wheeler could have done that. It's possible that it was cow-shaped, but there was nothing nearby that could have made it.

Just then, he heard a lowing come from deeper in the forest. It was getting dark, but the sound was not far away. That had clearly been a cow's voice.

His loafers splashed in the shallow mud as he dashed across the stream. The noise did not sound again, but he followed the direction from whence it came. After getting stabbed by several more snapping branches, he arrived at its source. He would never forget what he saw in the pine grove.

Lying on the moss-covered ground, he saw two cows on their left side, heads lying limp on the ground. Their breathing was labored and deliberate, one of their bellies scarred up, as if it had been split open and crudely fastened shut. He walked closer to them, his eyes fixed on the travesty in front of him. He saw caked blood on both of their foreheads, just above their eyes. Their dull cow eyes stared off, barely blinking, completely unfocused. They looked to be paralyzed, as they just lay there when the priest approached.

The sun was practically gone, the woods dark, with only a hint of reddish light still there to highlight the silent shades of trees. Father Matthew clicked on his flashlight and shone it around the area. He found that he was standing in the midst of a profuse mushroom grove, the kind that rise up like a church steeple, brown with black spots protruding off the caps. Father Matthew had not seen this kind before, so he stared more closely at the cap of the largest one near him. As he stared at it, he noticed that one of the black spots oozed before his eyes. It wasn't coloration: it was blood. The mushrooms were sprinkled with drying blood.

Father Matthew startled straight up when he heard a snap in the darkened wood. He searched around, the heavy breathing of the cattle covering up the smaller noises of the forest by night. As his flashlight searched fervently around the grove, it caught on a yellow t-shirt with one of those annoying stuffed puppets from the TV show on it. It was that little kid they kept showing on the TV news shows. He sat up against the base of a tree, a fine dusting of pine needles on him.

Father Matthew rushed over to the little boy, kneeling down to help him. "Son, are you alright? Everybody's been looking for you all over the county. What are you doing out here?" he asked, as he flicked the pine needles off the child. He wanted to make sure no bugs were on the kid, and he was also looking for injuries or signs of blood.

"Hey, let's get you out of here," he said. He stopped what he was doing when he saw the indentation in the boy's forehead. There was caked blood under the boy's nose, and his eyes stared, unfocused straight ahead of him.

"Oh my God," thought Father Matthew, "what happened to this child?" He was scratched up all over, and the web-like scabs covered the boy. What the hell was going on?

Whatever it was, Father Matthew needed to get him out of here. He and Mr. Pickles could come back tomorrow for the cows, but this boy needed help now. Picking the boy up over one shoulder, Matthew stood up right, the blood rushing to his head, making him unsteady. The exhaustion was really starting to tell on him.

As the priest turned to backtrack his path through the black woods, he jumped back, almost slipping to the ground as he yelped at what his flashlight illuminated. Just a few feet away in the grove stood what looked like a mud doll, barely two feet-tall. It stared at the priest who shone the flashlight right into its smooth, nose-less face, with burning coal-red, hate-filled eyes. It tilted its head to the side, like an animal measuring up prey, and let out a guttural hiss, opening its tiny mouth, filled with rows of rough, needle-like teeth. It had no ears, and it had stout, jagged claws instead of fingers, but what was most disturbing was its lone piece of clothing: on top of the thing's head was piled a coiled hat, made of what looked to be dried intestines.

Just then, a "POP" sounded, and the flashlight went out. The sun was down. And the priest found himself in the company of what people from the Old Country would have called an ettercap, whose grove he had invaded. But Americans don't have any legends about those creatures, and we don't cotton to superstitious clap-trap like that here anyway. It would be the most memorable night of Father Matthew Dunnigan's life.

In a terror-fueled night of sharp pain and desperate screaming, Matthew experienced what must be the torments of the damned. He ran as far as he could with the child, but lost him after tripping over a fallen branch. As he scrambled about for the child's still-breathing body, he grabbed onto the boy's leg, only to have it pulled from his grip by an incredibly awful strength. He dove in the dark after the boy's fleeing body, planting both hands in a death grip on the leg freshly wrested from him.

While he heard an uncomfortable pop in his ankle still caught in the log behind him, he couldn't be moved, and he struggled with every muscle in his body to hold onto the boy. The boy's body went limp a couple times as the thing jerked on some unseen limb, and finally slackened as the ettercap let go. Matthew had no time to take a breath, pulling himself free of the fallen limb and limping to his feet, as he snatched up the boy and began hobbling away.

He tripped in the stream where he saw the sign of the cows being dragged through the leaves, falling face-first into the mud. His vestment soaked with muck and leaf gut, he wiped his eyes as clean as he could, futile as that was in the dark. He rolled to one side to affect his rise and was launched onto his back, an irresistible force pulling him from behind. He slammed his head against a fallen limb and felt the boy's body be wrenched out of his grasp. Stunned by the impact, he lay there, as he heard the boy being dragged at an incredible pace away from the site, deeper into the forest.

It took a moment for his body to answer him, his eyes having flashed with black spots, even in the darkness. He pulled himself back up, his ankle now on fire with searing pain. He began hobbling away, but the ettercap's ire had been aroused. Now he would play his games with the wounded human.

Smoldering and screaming, Father Matthew Dunnigan ran his tattered body away from the flames that engulfed the woods behind him. His bloody eyelids seeped into his eyes, burning and blinding him, but he had somehow found enough kerosene and spite to set the woods on fire from deep inside. Oh, he had made it out of the woods and away from the claws of that little evil thing, but he wasn't going to let that be the end of it, even for one round. He had made it into the Pickles' pasture, broke into the barn, and grabbed all the flammable fuel he could set his stinging, lacerated hands on. Then he stumbled as fast as his hate would carry him back to the woods. He'd burn the little bastard out and take that sick grove with it.

As he stood at the edge of the forest raging with fire as the sun dawned in the east, he didn't notice the flashing blue lights or Mr. Pickles trying to talk him down. He didn't notice the hand-cuffs being put on him, or the emergency technicians try to close the hundreds of jagged, tiny cuts covering his body. He was charged with arson, and he stood trial for it. But they would never believe what new Hell he saw that night.

Legendary
By Joseph Tate

No shit, there I was.

If you've never looked straight down the barrel of a shotgun, picking a dude who wants to take everything you got isn't the way to make it happen. As a matter of fact, it can ruin your life. But me? Nah, not for me. The rest of that legendary night did that for me.

It all started with a seven day pass from Camp Pendleton, California. See, back then I was in the Marines, and I was probably one of the shittiest Marines you'd ever seen, but this story isn't about me. It's about the horrific things that happened to me in Memphis on that seven day pass that went on for nine days.

It all was going according to plan: I was driving my beat-up, ratty, old Volkswagon from California to visit my sister in Memphis, where I had grown up for several years. After Memphis, I was headed up to Wisconsin to visit some more family and friends, and then over to Virginia to visit friends at my previous duty station. Yeah, all of that, on a seven day pass, driving my piece of shit car, and getting back to California by Sunday. What could go wrong with a plan like that? Don't mind that right now, because that's another story.

So I showed up in Memphis, but not the nice part of town (and there is one). I had gone to visit my sister, who works for the IRS and is bat-shit crazy. I rolled up to her house in the hood (of which there's a baker's dozen), but this particular hood was south of Orange Mound.

Now I don't know if you've ever been to Orange Mound or known anything about it, but that's as far south in Memphis the white people want to go. Basically, the moment you go south of Southern Avenue, that's when you stop seeing white

99

people. There are people down there who almost never see white people in person, just on TV. Orange Mound was the first black subdivision made by blacks in the country, and it showed. In 1994, Orange Mound was rated by crime statistics to be the most violent neighborhood of Memphis, which is habitually one of the most dangerous places in the country. So let that paint the picture in your mind of where this story is going.

So I knocked on the door to my sister's shotgun shack, but didn't have to wait long. She immediately opened the door, and I smiled at her, opening my arms up for a big brother-sister hug.

"Oh, hey, Joseph. What are you doing here?" she said, as she used the screen door to brush past my welcoming embrace.

"I'm here to see my sister, dummy!" I joked at her. God, she was going to blow me off again, I could tell.

She stopped clipping in an earring to look confused at me. She slowly said, "Oh, Joseph, I thought you were coming in tomorrow. I've got a date with my girls tonight. I'm sorry."

I stood there quietly, but I gave up on the hug invitation. Bitch.

"I was just leaving," she said, her painted up lips flapping. "You want to hang out with Sylvester? He's here and ain't got nothing to do."

"Who the hell is that?"

"Oh, he's my boyfrien'," she smiled.

"You mean that jobless, good for nothing you've been bangin'?" I asked.

She pawed at me, then ducked her head back into the house. "SLY! I'm gonna go. My brother Joe is in town. Why don't you show him around?"

"Yup," was the muffled answer from inside the house.

"Alright, y'all have fun," my sister said, as she walked to her car, leaving me with some jack-wagon I had never met.

I sighed. I drove 1,800 miles for this? At least I had some ass waiting for me in Virginia, and some that was worth crawling to the moon for. Resigned, I opened the door to meet my host for the evening.

Sitting on the couch was a scrawny black dude, but he didn't look any more shady than anybody else in this town. For instance, he only had one gold toof (I know how you spell "tooth", and I know how he pronounced it), and he dressed in early 90s casual you might see anyplace else: a pair of jeans, a white undershirt with an unbuttoned plaid dress shirt over it, and a backward-turned ball cap. He didn't look up from an episode of "Fresh Prince" when I came in and the screen door slammed behind me.

I walked up to the edge of the couch in the slightly mildewed living room. Sly didn't look up. I waited.

It was already nine at night, and Sly was apparently alright with me waiting longer, so I caved and broke the ice.

"Hey, Sly. What's going on?"

Not looking up, he answered back plainly, "Oh, nothing much. What's up with you?"

"I just drove in from Camp Pendleton, California to see my sister, and she dumped me on you."

"That's kinda cold."

"Yeah. She's raggedy."

"You got that right."

"So what's there to do in this town?"

Sly thought for a minute, still watching Carleton trying to prove he was right, in vain. "Well, I need to do some laundry. You got a car?"

"Yeah, but I-"

101

"Good, cuz my license got suspended. Let me get my dirty, and I'll tell you where the laun-dro-mat is at."

Damn it. I ain't got any place else to stay or people to see in town, so I guess my Friday night will be taking my sister's dead-beat boyfriend to do his laundry. Argh.

Sly came out of the bedroom with a duffle bag of laundry and stopped to scratch his bristly chin. "You got any you need doing?" he asked.

"I guess. But I don't have any money on me."

"That's okay. I know a place we can get some rolls of quarters this time of night."

So we rolled around the hood in my ghetto sled and stopped in to see an old man about some quarters. Two rolls of quarters in hand (all thanks to my wallet), we sputtered to a stop in front of the stooped laundromat, its dull fluorescent lights shining out onto the busted, cracked asphalt parking lot. We could see through the full-length windows that we would be the only people in there, but hey, not everybody knows how to rock the night like we did.

Since we had the place to ourselves, we walked in like champs and claimed the first loaders we found. Breaking open the first roll of quarters, we pushed the lever and listened to the hiss of beat-up washers get to work. I walked around the place to see if there were any posters on the wall saying something, anything, was going on tonight so I could ditch Sly and do some partying. Sly slid down into one of those hard, plastic chairs bolted to the ground, apparently feeling no compulsion to entertain his charge for the evening.

I found no community board or crappy posters saying, "Come see my shitty band! (BYOB)", so I guessed that staring at the washer swirl was going to be the best thing to happen to me tonight. Well, at least I'd be able to get a move on earlier than planned for Wisconsin, where I had more than one flaky nut-bag waiting for me. Sly sat for a bit, then took off to walk a few blocks to get something cold and frosty while we waited. Towards the end of the wash cycle, I was headed over to a scuffed up chair when the door swung open and my night got interesting.

In through the door came two jacked up crack-heads, wearing all kinds of mismatched sweaters and vests all wrong. They had one arm in a sleeve here, but got distracted before they put the other sleeve on, so they just put on another garish, ripped up something on over the off arm to make up for it. Only crack-heads dress like that, because no other drug makes people think dressing like that looks good. And their faces were all screwed up, like their cheek and eyebrow muscles had a seizure and forgot to go back to normal. How could this not go someplace awesome?!

"HHEeeeYY!" the one with a toboggan hollered (never mind it was warm outside, but I guess his hair was cold), at no one in particular. His eyes were bloodshot, he stank like he hadn't washed in a week, he was missing teeth, and he turned to look at me.

I looked straight back, unimpressed. I dealt with crack-heads before: just make some loud noises and say you see the cops, and they should run off. If you feel like being charitable, just give him the quarter he asks for.

"Gimme all yo' money," he slurred. I noticed the two were shaking, whether from withdrawal or adrenaline I couldn't tell.

"Plum out," was all I said.

That seemed to throw him. He turned to his partner and flashed him a "now what?" look.

The crack-heads turned to face me, "I said gimme yo' money, asshole," ordered the talkative one. His friend started bobbing on the balls of his feet for no reason.

"Listen, just go on and get. I put my last quarters in the machine," I countered.

Just then the quiet one pulled out from under his layers of jackets a single-barrel shotgun and pointed it straight at my face. Well, shiiiiiiit…

I held my hands up and started talking. I'd had guns pointed and fired at me before, but this was point-blank and over some damn quarters. It'd be more trouble than it was worth to not just hand it over.

"Aight, aight, I got you. This is all I got," I said, fishing out the opened and sealed rolls of coins out of my pockets. I held them out to Chatty McCrack-Head, then held my hands up so they didn't freak out any more than they already were.

Chatty giggled like a school-girl when he counted the quarters, and his partner leered in a drooling smile when he saw it. After Chatty crammed them in one of his many pockets, his face turned angry.

"Gimme everything you got!"

"I just gave you all my money."

"Take your clothes off!"

Aight. I was done with this bullshit. I sat down in one of those hard as rocks chair and kicked back, telling them, "Now, boys, you best get ta getting. I'm through with you."

Chatty thought for a moment. The moment was in no hurry to leave, though, so we stood at an impasse.

"Aight," Chatty concluded. "Gimme yo' clothes you is washin'!"

"You want my wet clothes?"

"I SAID GIVE IT!" Chatty screamed, while Shotgun pointed the barrel closer to my face.

I just shook my head and headed over to the washing machines. Shotgun followed me as I went, watching me like a hawk as I stopped the rinse cycle. The fact that I thought this was the dumbest thing I had ever been held up for didn't stop me from opening the washer and grabbing my soaking wet, dirty clothes.

I started to put the sopping wet clothes into Sly's duffel bag, when Chatty shouted, "Don't do that! Hand 'em over!"

Whatever. I gave him handful after handful of wet laundry, the water splashing down onto the dirty, tiled floor as I did so. When the deed was done, Chatty practically glowed with pride.

Without a further word, the two backed out of the laundromat, keeping the shotgun up to warn me against trying anything. I didn't even have my hands up anymore; I was disgusted by the shittiness of the stick-up that just went down.

See, both crack and cocaine come from the same basic drug, coca leaves. White people with money go for cocaine, but black people go for crack, and I think you can chalk up why black people got it so much worse than white people to the effects of the two drugs. Cocaine makes you feel invincible and like you can conquer the world, so investment bankers, big business guys, and white artists and musicians go balls to the wall to make something big happen. Crack makes you do stupid shit like what just happened and prove why we can't have nice things in the hood.

So there I was, wet and broke from handing everything I had on me to a couple of crack-heads at a ghetto laundromat. I was ready to call it a night, and then Sly walked back in with a freshly opened brew and not a care in the world.

"You ready to go, Sly?" I asked.

"Go where?"

"Go home. I'm done for the night."

Sly reacted in shock. "What do you mean, 'go home'? It's only ten o'clock."

My annoyance becoming evident, I said, "Sly, I just got held up for your laundry and my quarters. That's a tough act to follow."

"DAMN, Joseph," he paused, thinking. "Don't worry about it man, we'll make it happen."

"Sure," I said in resignation and snatched his beer away from him, chugging it down. I was pissed off and wanted something to distract me.

So I drove Sly over to his parents' supermarket so he could get the key to the house (what parents lock their grown son out of the house? Smart ones). You know, I apologize, this wasn't really a grocery store: this was a front. It was a false façade, a fake store used to sell drugs in the open. How did I know this was a front? Because the small store only had wilted produce, antique cans of expired and bloated stuff on the shelves, dust on the counters, no grocery carts, and it was open 24 hours a day. Does that sound like a place people go looking for cuts of meat? Hell no.

I just stood by the counter while Sly went to find his parents in the back of the store, and I didn't see another soul come in. I heard some distant shouting from inside the store, but hey, it wasn't coming my way and it didn't have a shotgun, so I didn't give a fuck. About ten minutes later, my sister's boyfriend came back my way looking perturbed, but ready to go.

Burning my gas again, we made it to his house. It was a typical low-rent affair with peeling paint and bars on the windows. The first thing that jumped out at me when we went inside was the acrid haze; the second was the sight of an incredible amount of Tupperware stacked all over the living room. I'm serious: there were stacks and stacks of Pyrex rising five feet high. Why would you need that many plastic containers? Because you're pushing weed and want to contain the smell, that's why!

Well, somebody was letting the ganja out of the bag big time, because the place reeked of high times. Sly walked in as I hesitated at the door, but then he motioned for me to follow him into the house, saying, "Come on, Soldier. I got some friends I want you to meet."

First off, I was a Marine, not a Soldier, but I let that slide. Second off, I didn't see any friends, Marines get drug tested all the time, and I was pretty sure what kind of friends Sly kept.

Reluctantly, I followed. When I passed from the paraphernalia-riddled living room to the den, I saw what friends Sly was talking about. Seated on the worn carpet were about a dozen people, just sitting around smoking weed. Then I realized the problem: not one of them could be over 15 years old. I paused in the doorway, frozen by the scene, until Sly bumped me, asking if I wanted in.

After seeing the haze of smoke they were pumping out and the number of felonies sitting in front of me, I knew this was a bad place for me to be. I'd been in trouble with the law enough on my own: I did not need this much help getting into more. Before Sly could introduce me around to everyone, I pulled him aside and told him I just wanted a drink to unwind. He made me wait long enough for him to get four big tokes in, but in a random act of consideration, he said he knew just the place to get down. No, I didn't sigh in exasperation out of knowing exactly what kind of classy joint Sly was going to take me to, because at this point I didn't care.

I should have. Sly took me to a bar in downtown Memphis, but I ain't talking about those clean, friendly, unlikely to get raided by the cops bars on Beale Street where all the respectable people get drunk in public. Oh, no: we went to a run-down, shotgun junt (that's "joint" or "place" to you white people) about three blocks north of the nice part of downtown.

I've been some dark and dirty places, but in Memphis, there's a kind of black in the night you just can't find anywhere else. Sly walked me through that darkness to get to the door of the place, because it was so broke-down that there weren't any lights on the outside to let you know it was open.

Once I got inside, I found out why. The first thing I saw was two dudes at a table, right in front of the door mind you, counting out crack rocks. Why, I don't know; maybe they were trying to figure out how many to take now and save for later. But I did see a bar with a refrigerator full of beer behind it, so it wasn't my problem.

I ordered the first of many beers and finally started to relax for the night. I mostly talked to Sly, because I don't really like people, and I really didn't want to get caught up in a tough-man contest with one of these hood rats when they found out I was a Marine. But, you know, after three beers, Sly got to be not such an intolerable shitbag, so the night was picking up. We got to smoking and joking about the crack-heads that robbed us of our dirty clothes earlier, and the time started to fly.

We were still bullshitting when I happened to glance up and see the clock on the wall turning to midnight. I wouldn't have thought anything of it, but at that moment, the bartender grabbed this big bell from behind the counter and rang that shit like an epileptic possessed. Everything got quiet, as two guys nearest the front and back doors moved over and locked those things up. Another man went over to the jukebox, slid a quarter in, and put on an old Bill Withers track.

That's when my night, maybe even my life, went to shit. The twenty or so lowlifes in the bar started hollering in unison and standing up, which was weird. But then the nasty hos that were there started taking off all their clothes and grinding on everybody within grinding distance. I'm talking C-section scars, stab scars, bullet scars, needletracks (on the arms and the toes), wigs coming off, false teeth coming out, you name it: if it turned your stomach, these hos had it.

Struggling to keep my beer down, I couldn't believe what Sly said to me next. "Hey, man: wi'ontch you get you some of that? I told you I had something for ya," he said with a greasy grin.

"Help myself to what?" I answered, shock in my voice.

"Check it, Joe. This is a thang all the pimps do every week. Let everybody get a taste of the goods, you know what I'm sayin'."

I was seriously about to throw up: I was at a pimp swap-meet. I had before me a veritable buffet of slutty, female ass, but I ain't talking no all you can eat champagne and lobster: I'm talking a hogs knuckles and chittlins buffet.

I had to leave; I had to get out of here. The smell of rotten, stanky pussy, the greasy bastard essence in the air, the beer that suddenly wasn't sitting too well in my gut: it all added up to the last straw in one miserable, fucking night.

I remember trying to leave, but the doors were locked and weren't nobody getting out. All I could do was sit there and watch in disgust and terror as the ghetto-nastiness unfolded and Sly snuck in to get his. I had to find some way out of the reach of the skanks when they made their rounds near me, trying desperately to avoid their STD-laden, cracked fingernails. Something in my face must have let them hos know that I wasn't down for the ground brown.

I remember telling the dude at the door to, "Open it, or I'm taking it off the frame." I was free at last. You can't unlive that kind of night; you can't unsee what I've seen.

Left Alone
By JT Davenport

Whitehaven, just south of Downtown, 1957

Now, as everyone knows, boys will be boys, and some boys act like fiends on a jailbreak from Hell, but most of the little guys usually outgrow this phase. Not always, though. They will misbehave and do all sorts of mean things like pulling puppy dogs' tails, set fire to ants, steal lunch money, etc. Typically, a whollop on the behind would cure the problem, but not in this case. This was one time when the retribution that was well-deserved was actually served. Let me introduce Lawrence, who was cut from a crueler cloth.

Lawrence was small, but you might say he was filled with a mean spirit. At a tender age, he delighted in terrorizing the neighborhood stray dog, a sweet-natured white and black mutt, to the point where the dog would run and hide. Lawrence always found him and kept up his cruel games with the little mutt, unless he found something else he could "play" with.

One day, Lawrence found several butterflies and promptly pulled their wings off, and then their heads. Heaven help them if they could still feel anything after that, because he would then jump on them while their bodies were still quivering, so he could make them go "squish". Beetles would go "pop", since they had harder bodies. That was a very pleasing sound to little Lawrence.

A couple of weeks later, the little hellion discovered matches and what you could do with them. He even managed to find something that burned when you lit it to pour on the caterpillars he found in a wooden shed on an abandoned lot. They were big bugs, blue and red-banded with two large, golden-colored horns sticking off the end of their tails. So he decided to light them up. When they caught on fire, he was overjoyed to see the helpless little critters feverishly wiggle about, desperate to keep living. Lawrence did his little victory dance and stomped on them when the flames died down.

But the caterpillars came back the next day, and the day after that as well. Little Lawrence was simply ecstatic with joy. He lit them up, watched them burn, and did his little victory dance over their ruined corpses.

Then on the fourth day of his reign of terror, the caterpillars had come back, but apparently they were trying to leave the shack a bit early to get away from Lawrence, and he almost missed them. He found them just as the last one was going down a large hole in the ground, being about a foot around.

Well, he wasn't going to allow himself to be denied his victory this day, and since he'd already forgotten about the dog, he wanted his caterpillars to die in horrid agony, and he wanted them to die in horrid agony right now! So he got down on his little knees and began to dig with his hands. The earth was soft and flakey, so there was no problem for him to make headway in enlarging the hole with his bare hands.

He got so involved with his digging that he didn't realize that he was now inside the hole he made, and a good way down at that. He also failed to notice that most of the day had long since passed, and night was fast approaching. The light was fading, and it was nearly pitch black inside his hole. He could see the caterpillars just out of reach below him, because they were glowing. He stopped what he was doing, raptly transfixed by this latest revelation.

He'd never seen anything this beautiful, so he watched them move about at the end of what he came to think of as his hole. They moved back and forth, and eventually moved out through small holes in the sides of the hole, down by the end. He lost sight of them for a while, as he lay there in the dirt, contemplating what they would look like and sound like when he stomped on them this time.

Suddenly, he felt something on his back, and then more of them, and more. It was the caterpillars, he was certain of that, but he couldn't turn around or roll over, because the hole just wasn't big enough for him to do that!

The caterpillars burrowed out of a hundred little tunnels in the hole Lawrence had dug for himself and spun their silk over him, again and again until little Lawrence couldn't be heard, let alone be seen. As the night stars came out, the caterpillars changed shape, gallivanting off in a fairy ride under the stars. And, little Lawrence was never seen or heard from again!

Bumpi Takes Over
By Stephen Clements

"Give me yo' money!" threatened the hood rat, as he flipped open a gleaming knife under the dim street light flickering on and off on South Parkway. The flashing of the light glistened off the moist, fake gold teeth of the young black man, as he moved within cutting distance of his victim.

The man he stared down was blacker still, with jet black skin that had been cured in the cruel sun lording over people who lived on the Equator. Under his thread-bare hoody, Bumpi felt his blood rush, and he felt it all the more when the thug's two friends stepped out behind him from the shadowy driveway walls they had used for concealment.

Bumpi Obajawe knew suffering. He spent his first 22 years in the Democratic Republic of the Congo, which one reliable news source described, charitably, as: "A hellscape of death and human misery." Bumpi was the second youngest of seven kids, brought up by their fleeing mother. She had fled the river valley for the eastern Congo, because Bumpi's father had been hacked to death with machetes on his little brother's first birthday. A dozen armed men from a neighboring tribe visited Bumpi's village when they learned of the birthday celebration, demanding the young boy's birthday presents as ransom for sparing his family's lives. They wouldn't believe Bumpi's dad when he said that there weren't any, so they hacked him limb from limb, and then they raped his mother and sisters, none older than 14.

Two of Bumpi's sisters disappeared after the family had fled east, looking for UN peacekeepers in the hopes of being safe with them. He thinks he found his sisters' skulls and shattered bones, covered with rotten flesh, when he was playing in a sewage ditch by himself one day. Three of his

113

brothers were killed at random, as they hid behind the jungle trees and were sprayed down with bullets by two opposing rebel groups. The peacekeepers weren't doing a very good job. The Ulungi, the taller rebel faction, ate one of Bumpi's playmates alive, believing that pygmies had magical powers you could gain by eating them.

Bumpi himself spent most of his life near starvation, but other than almost dying in a rogue crocodile attack where some missionary doctors saved him from certain death, he was a lucky guy. When he got of age, he paid what little money he, his mother, and his younger brother could scrape together and prayed to whatever cruel gods existed for him to enter the US State Department's Visa Lottery program. Apparently, the gods were still full from the neighboring village having been burned to the ground and let him win.

The immigration officials decided that Bumpi should be settled in Memphis, after considering the ethnic diversity of the area (it was mostly black and poor), and the fact that the Iraqis they settled there from their war-torn country were doing well. They showed him pictures of this lush, green place with actual roads and houses that weren't all burned-out. It looked like a place Bumpi would like. At any rate, it wasn't the Congo, so off he went. He knew some halting English, which was still more than a lot of Memphians, but he wasn't prepared for the Promised Land he had been given. He hadn't even heard of Elvis.

But Bumpi knew what to do with some punk-bitches who wanted to take something that wasn't theirs. You grab the tree branch lying in the pile of refuse on the busted-up sidewalk, and you beat the shit out of them. The weak knick the first bitch gave him didn't even make Bumpi slow down the primordial ass-beating he laid down on the two he caught.

He didn't walk around armed: Bumpi didn't want to hurt anybody. But he knew if you start off with a stiff blow to the stomach and follow through with your whole body, that's getting off on the right foot. Not only is it a big target, but you knock all the wind out of your opponent, which usually makes them drop what they're holding and try to back up as fast as they can, in their desperate attempt to breathe.

When a wounded person is trying to back up on uneven ground, that's a great time to smash something really hard into their knee, because they are guaranteed to go down. Then you can turn around and smack the other guy in the face with the splintered, dry wood: it might not be a sure-fire killing blow, but nobody likes to have their face hit with sharp splinters, let alone get some in their eyes.

They try to back up, and at least one hand is going to try and protect their face. That's when you grab an elbow and pull it in an off direction, so they lose their footing and trip. While the other guy is scrambling away and happy to breathe again, you grab this one by the collar (baggy clothes are great for getting your ass beat) and drive his head into the concrete driveway wall. Better do it again, just to make sure it took.

The third guy is long gone at this point. He might have even dropped his weapon, as if that proves he's harmless or not a bad guy if the cops show up. Shocking as this revelation might be, people that try to rob other people are generally cowards. Surprising, I know.

Sure enough, the first guy had dropped his knife. Bumpi would pick it up later, but for now he just needed the tree branch to fly end over end and very fast into the back of the head of the first guy who thought he was safe, since he was swimming faster from the shark than his buddy. Not fast enough.

So, all told, the pay-off the three hood rats got from demanding Bumpi's money was: one had shit himself and run, one was blacked out with a concussion in the driveway, and the instigator had just broke his tooth on the crumbling sidewalk. Their night was about to get worse.

"IS THIS WHAT YOU WANT?" Bumpi yelled in his throaty voice straight into the bleeding face of the first fool to step up to the plate, as he lifted him inches off the ground by his collar.

"Naw, man. I wuz jus' axin' for direc-"

PUNCH.

"AWW, SHIT," came the muffled response to Bumpi's hard, bony fist.

"DO YOU THINK I AM THE STUPID? You threaten to cut me for money, and you think I am the bitch?" Bumpi screamed at his miserable prey. The street light flickered, as the leaf-heavy trees rustled in the breeze.

"Let me go, man," begged the bloody thug.

Bumpi shoved him back onto the concrete, watching his victim writhe from the protruding sidewalk biting into his back. Looking him up and down, Bumpi let his visceral rage lead his foot into the thug's head a few times, before Bumpi decided it was time to fix this. Picking up the knife that was formerly pointed at him, he pulled the thug up, planting the blade at his throat.

"Now we go. You go to the police now. You will pay for what you do, evil man," he said, as he forced the crying thug towards the nearest house. The lights were on two doors down, and as they climbed the porch stoop, Bumpi threw him to the floor, keeping the knife pointed at him.

Bumpi knocked on the door, and the innards of the house went still. He knocked again.

"Who is it?" came the muffled Memphis drawl, hesitantly from inside.

"I need the police."

"They ain't hur."

"No, I need to call the police. I have two criminals out here to give to them."

The door opened up, and a tall, chunky black woman in dirty sweats looked at Bumpi and his charge. "Oh, Hell, naw! You need to take this someplace else, I don't need no cops comin' hur," she finished, an edge of indignation in her voice.

"Miss, this man and his friend tried to rob me. I need help to send them to the police." Bumpi was a little confused at having to explain this.

"Listen, young buck, whateva problem you got, you needs to be taking it somewhere else. I got enough troubles, so get on." She slammed the door.

Bumpi stared incredulously at the door, his attention only shifting when he heard chuckling from the floor of the porch. Looking down, he saw the grinning face of the thug at his feet.

"Du', po-po don't roll in this neighbuhood! You best let my ass go."

PUNCH.

Bumpi was furious. He could see that the thug was right, and how many houses did he want to drag a bloodied robber to, hoping somebody would call the cops? Things were supposed to be different in America. People were supposed to follow laws, and the police were supposed to do more than take bribes to turn a blind eye to crimes.

"Y'all need to get off my porch," came a muffled holler from inside the dilapidated, white house.

Okay, Bumpi could take care of this. He had heard of 201 Poplar, the prison. He would drag him to the law, if the law would not come here.

At knife point, Bumpi forced the criminal to begin walking. He left the other one with his head in the wall. Two miles into their rather strained walk, Bumpi's heart soared when he saw a police car driving down the street towards them. He waved furiously with his free hand and was pleased to see the blue lights on the top of the car start rolling.

The thug made one last attempt to escape when he turned to run, but Bumpi was wise to his tricks. A swift stomp on the back of his calf was all it took to put an end to that. Bumpi knew how to smell stupidity.

The smell got stronger as the car pulled up. The windows rolled down, revealing two sleepy, overweight officers, one high-yellow and one mocha colored, glancing out the window. The thought of getting out of the car was clearly off the table.

"What's going on here?" asked the speckled, high-yellow driver through his thick mustache. In the passenger seat, his droopy-jawed, mocha companion was only too happy to leave his attention out of this.

"Officer," Bumpi began, "this man and two of his friends attacked me with a knife to try to rob me. I have brought this one to you, and the other is lying on the street a short distance away. Arrest this one, and I will take you to the other."

The driver stared blankly at the two young men standing in the street next to his car. The wrinkles around his glassy-eyes didn't even budge when he asked, "What for?"

"These men tried to rob me, and they will do it again!" Bumpi was getting fed up with having to explain to people why it was a good idea for violent criminals to be dealt with by the law. Especially, he saw, to officers of the law.

"Listen, I didn't see anything happen, and now I just see you holding a knife to a chewed-up dude. You should have called the police when it happened. I got nothing on this guy, but I could find something on you for holding a knife to him," the driver finished, his power window beginning to whirr back upwards.

Bumpi charged the car, pushing his palms down on the tinted window before it closed. "YOU ARE MEN OF THE LAW! WHY DO YOU NOT DO YOUR JOB?!"

The window stopped momentarily. The officer in the passenger seat had a twinkle in his eye that might have meant he was going to get involved. It passed. He sipped what was in his coffee cup instead.

The driver looked up at Bumpi's face, not looking with enough intent to actually look him in the eyes. "Get your hands off the car, boy. And get off the crack."

Bumpi's long face twisted in incredulity and then surprise as the car drove away, the window finishing its journey by the end of the block. He stared after it, mouth agape in disbelief. Then he heard the snickering again. Then he heard the blood-curdling shriek that came with an angrily hurled knife finding its mark.

Bumpi couldn't believe this. He left one country where the police, or the peacekeepers, or the random gendarme did nothing actually related to their job, but to come to America, to the oft-touted best country in the world, and to see the same crap going on! How did this country get this far with laws enforced like this!

When the police car turned down a side street and disappeared from view, he decided to check back on his robber, since the police didn't want him.

Rather than take the opportunity to run from the immigrant that had just hurled his own knife into him without even looking, the thug gave up and was lying on the ground, knife in right bicep, crying. Again with the crying!

Bumpi stalked over to his prey. If the cops wouldn't settle this, he would. "Who do you work for?"

"Wuh?"

KICK.

"WHO DO YOU ROB PEOPLE FOR?"

It became abundantly clear to the man on the ground that he should say, "Fuck it," and tell this angry African whatever he wanted to know. The current plan was not working. "Maaan, you ain't got shit on him. But since you done good on yo' bidness wif me," he coughed, "and I'm stuck on the ground, fuck it, I'll tell you."

He struggled to sit up, in vain. He motioned for Bumpi to help him up against the trunk of the thick tree breaking through the sidewalk, and Bumpi complied. The thug pulled out a pack of Lucky Strikes and lit up. "Nigga, this goes to the top. No shit, I drove my loke-dog one night downtown, and I saw da mayor come out wif him."

The mayor? The ruler of this city? Things weren't any damn different here! "Where can I find him? This will not go on any longer."

"Nigga, you dumb as OOOWWW!!!"

It's good to be the king. Sometimes. But not in Memphis. We kill our kings here.

That's why the reigning monarch, er, mayor of the city settled on being a duke. He was called Duke Willie, and he ran this city like his own personal fiefdom. Straight into the ground, as hard as he could ram it. There were whole sections of the city, a sprawling monstrosity that almost covered an entire county, that were derelict now, but used to be thriving, productive communities when he came to power.

Hickory Hill had been a nice, working-class neighborhood with a good mall and lots of hot, new stores opening all the time. But Duke Willie couldn't stand that the white people had a nice place to live where they didn't have to pay his tribute, er, taxes. So he told a judge that the city of Memphis could provide the public services Hickory Hill needed (which apparently consisted of a library and a community center), and a few thousand dollars later, the judge agreed. One more neighborhood fell to the "plague of locusts"-effect Memphis has on its new territories.

This had happened all over Shelby County: a nice community sprang up, people fled to it from the war-zone level of crime and violence found in the Memphis city limits, Duke Willie got upset that the white people found another place to hole up, annexed them, and then the place fell apart as it was swarmed with ghetto trash and the gangs that moved with them. Watch, rinse, weep.

Memphis is a big city with a lot of people and a lot of money, but those who have it do a great job of hiding it from those who want to carjack it. Basically, there is a thin band of the city from the Mississippi going east along Walnut Grove and Poplar Avenue that is habitable, some parts even nice, and vast, dark hell mouths to the north and south of it. When it looked like Willie was going to lose the first election that made him Duke, he threatened to incite race riots that would set the city on fire if a recount was called for by his white, incumbent opponent. These are the places his hordes would come from.

Willie liked it that way. In those festering cesspools of humanity, he ruled through his people, the "REAL PEOPLE" he was so fond of calling on (which are actually the ghetto hustlers he used to run his network), and in the nice parts of the city, he could go enjoy his ill-gotten gains.

What Willie didn't like, though, was somebody was fucking with his money. His street-level agents kept showing up in the freeholds of Germantown and Collierville at the police station, with bulging bags of weed and heroin sticking out of their pockets, bound, bloodied, and gagged with duct tape. This was a major problem, because he couldn't just have his boys at the Memphis PD steal the evidence and let their non-uniformed associates go with a fine they would never pay. Those bastards in Germantown and Collierville actually arrested people for breaking the law, out of their misguided sense of duty to protect their communities from crime.

Pointing his lit cigar at his watery-eyed toady from high atop his throne in his office, the open windows letting in breeze that fluttered the golden curtains around him as though he were a black Zeus, Duke Willie passed down his commandment. "I don't care how much it costs, Devon, I want the mother fucker who's fucking with my bidness dead. What part of that don't you understand?" The light paneling of the room reverberated with the thick, almost nasal resonance of his powerful voice.

Devon, an uninspiring whipping boy, nodded his head, as he shifted in his loafers back and forth on the carpet. "Yezzuh, boss, I got dat. But I tellz ya again: we can't find da guy. Our peoples don't see da Memphis Mafia anywhere around dis, so we'z still lookin'. Money ain't da issue, boss."

"LISTEN TO ME, MOTHA FUCKA," erupted the Duke, rising like Lucifer clawing his way out of Hell from his high-backed tan leather chair, "I WANT YO' ASS OUT THERE LOOKIN' FOR THIS ASSHOLE THEN! I want you to paint a mutha fuckin' sign on yo' black ass sayin', 'I sell crack for Duke Willie', just to see if you can get this guy to punk yo' ass. Jus' make sho' you got some back-up waitin' to beat his ass when you do!"

Devon needed a change of clothes.

Willie relaxed, his fury taken out on somebody. He stood there, the burning Churchill in his right hand, as he raised his left to scratch at the short white hair on his scalp. "Listen, just go get with Thomas and see what you can find," he finished, kicking back into his reclining chair.

"Yezzuh, boss," croaked Devon, sweat beading up along his scrubby black mustache. He turned on his heels to leave, and this time he'd find somebody to pin this on. Fuck if he was going to get shot by his boss like he was last time this shit went down.

"Man, that looks painful," Devon thought to himself. The hollow thump of the lead pipe coming down on the human bait's back sounded as bad as it looked to Devon, as he watched the scene unfold through the bullet hole in the cinder-block wall of the abandoned gas station. Devon was not about to have that happen to him, so he set up a decoy drug-hustler to see if they could bring out the punk that was meddling with Duke Willie's business. It worked.

He watched the lanky African hopping like a mad rabbit, a broken chair leg swinging down on the unconscious sap on the floor. Devon was waiting for this guy to get comfortable, to quiet down before he and his boys sprung the trap. It took a while.

When Bumpi cast the leg down to catch his breath, Devon motioned for his boys to move in. As Bumpi knelt down to start hog-ducting the fall guy, he heard the loafers of four shady men shuffle into the place. They came in from two different entrances, surrounding Bumpi. As he stood to face this new threat, Bumpi recognized one from the Nation of Islam office that tried to give him some bean cola. It was terrible.

There were no words exchanged. His pulse quickening and the sweat beading on his oily skin, Devon pointed and yelled, "Get him!"His hired muscle sprang into action, brandishing different weapons as Devon ran to the back of the room. Duke Willie wanted this bastard alive, so no guns were drawn.

That was a small comfort for Bumpi, as three professionals ambushing you after you've done wore yourself out way-laying a punk bitch is not a recipe for success. I could detail the fight sequence, but at this point in the story, we both like Bumpi, and I wouldn't want it on either of our consciences that we sat here and read about our immigrant friend taking a beating like it was his job without at least trying to help. So, for both our sakes, let's just say, "A vicious, short melee ensued, and Bumpi came up short. Devon noted to change his boxers later, but for now he'd avoided being beaten for screwing up Duke Willie's orders."

"Dat's right, put him in the car," puffed Devon, as he wiped the blood and sweat from his face. He thought he would be safe at the back of the room, but that African bastard was scrappy.

A passing hobo in a dingy hoodie stood outside the wrecked gas station and watched, as the three men stumbled out of what was left of the building. They carried Bumpi out to the car, leaving the unconscious vigilante-bait on the floor, amidst the debris.

"Man, wooo! You licked his ass good!" squealed the toothless hobo. "Got any smokes?"

Devon brushed him aside, telling him, "Go home."

"I am home!"

"Go someplace else." Devon made it to the car first, and as he was fishing for his keys, he noticed that the driver side tires lay as flat as a gutted squirrel on the asphalt.

"Fuck! God damn it, them motha fuckas! If I find out who did this, I'm gonna kill me a mutha-", he spat out before being cut off.

An elderly gentleman had stepped out from the overgrown bushes by the sidewalk, walking stick in hand. He looked appraisingly at the situation, what with the torn suits and unconscious African being hoisted into the trunk of the old Town Car. Stating the obvious, the old man said, "You got a problem."

"Go home, old man. We got it," said Devon dismissively, not even looking at the gentleman. He could call somebody to come fix this. No biggie. Duke Willie still got what he wanted tonight.

"No, I was telling you, you got a problem," said Blind Apricot Harding, as his walking stick brought down the first thug wrestling to stuff Bumpi's lanky body into the trunk.

Devon watched as his hired man went down like a high school chick after one wine cooler, shock flashing across his face. He backed up, his loafers scuffing across the road, as his hands feverishly went through his pockets looking for a weapon. His horror increased, as he saw a dozen men step out of the shadows, surrounding him and his men. The Teahouse gang was about to strike. The pain was brought with a quickness.

"I LOVE COCAINE!!!" bellowed the Duke in his fiefdom, as he pulled up from his third line in the club. At first, he clenched his eyes with a strength that could have cut diamonds, but when he opened them, he saw the scintillating disco ball illuminate his world. He'd seen this heaven of paid-for-women and R&B lit up like that before, which is why he kept doing it.

"Oh my God, hahahahaha," he trailed off, as he covered his face with one of his giant palms. He was tripping balls. It was great. Through the din of music and joy, he started hearing this annoying sound, though.

It was a quiet, insistent voice. "Sir. Sir. Sir," it went.

As the initial rush eased into the high he was already working with, Willie looked in the direction of the sound. It was one of the little server boys, dressed in his gaudy tuxedo. Who the fuck was this mortal to be bothering him?

"WHAT?" screamed the Duke, lurching across the table with his blood-shot eyes ablaze at the young man.

"Sir, I was asked to give this to you. It's good news, I was supposed to tell you," said the jerry-curled man, handing an envelope to his master.

Willie snatched it away jealously, to keep anybody else from having anything good in their lives. He tore it open and saw a Polaroid picture fall onto the cocaine and champagne-frosted table. "Ah, it must be proof of the capture," he thought. Devon couldn't very well bring that bastard in here.

Duke Willie squinted in the purplish light of the club, trying to make out the details of the black man in the picture. He didn't have his reading glasses on, so he turned to the light-skinned prostitute with straight hair next to him. "BITCH, CAN YOU SEE THIS? THE PICTURE'S BLURRY."

That very fine woman could make out the picture, and she covered her face to conceal her disgust when she recognized what it was.

"WHAT IS IT, BITCH?"

She choked down her rising champagne to answer. "It's yo' boy, Devon. Naked. Tied up, on your desk. It looks like a fat, chocolate mountain."

"BITCH, WHAT?!!!" Willie raged, his anger moving him to fling the waif across the table one-handed. Willie was not pleased.

"You alright, young blood?" came a voice, shaky at first. The second time Bumpi heard it, it was more real, less like

126

something in a dream. He opened his swollen eyes to see the fine caramel skin of the man who spoke the smooth baritone to him.

Leon's straight black hair and crisp white suit looked in perfect order. You'd never know he had just beat some serious ass in it.

Bumpi found himself lying on a roughed-up cot with a frayed sheet over him. He went to raise himself up, only to find his body so stiff he could only groan and lay back down.

"Cool down, cat," reassured Leon. "You're in a good place now. It might not look like much, but welcome to our office. It used to be a teahouse, but now the only tea we can offer you is the malt liquor kind."

Bumpi saw a tall, fat gentleman walking up behind Leon, carrying two wooden folding chairs. While he set them down, Bumpi looked around the place. It was in marginally better repair than the abandoned gas station he had just been in, but the spirit of the place was that of being lived in. It had a vitality to it, where the place he was beaten unconscious was dead and forlorn. Sure, this gang headquarters was rough, what with the bluish paint being worn off the floors, and the green paint on the walls mostly being held there by posters of women in bikinis, low-riders, and R&B greats, but something about it was cozy.

Leon helped the grizzled Blind Apricot Harding down onto one of the folding chairs, then took a seat himself. Bumpi saw other young men at the far side of the converted diner, but they kept their distance and their peace.

Leon struck a long, skinny match on the box and lit his Cools cigarette. "We're big fans of yours. What's your name?"

"My name is Bumpi Obajawe. I am new to Memphis."

"Bump, I'm Leon. This is Harding. Back there are some other dudes you'll meet later. The guy who jumped you was

Duke Willie's toad Devon, and I can tell you that he brought his best to take you down. I wish we had gotten there sooner, but you're safe now, and Duke Willie is not happy. Which makes us all very happy," he stopped to take a drag off his smoke. His lips barely showed it, but his eyes showed a rich smile.

He continued, "See, Bump, Harding and his crew and me and my crew had just settled things between us when we started hearing these wild stories about you. One by one, we heard of Duke Willie's 'real people' getting scooped off the streets like the trash they are. Nobody knew who was doing it, but they knew your face. Pretty soon, everybody's gonna know your face around here."

Bumpi's head throbbed. He decided to let this guy keep talking.

"See, Bump, M-town didn't used to be like this. We let it get here. This used to be a great place to be a black person in America trying to get ahead. Good people from all over the South used to come here to make sweet music, music so good even the white folk started doing it. There might be a lot of good music elsewhere, but Memphis done changed how everybody made everything sound good."

The old man next to him chimed in with his raspy voice, saying, "Not no more they don't. All the young bucks aspire to nowadays is chingy bullshit. Don't nobody play instruments; all they do is talk about how bad they are, how many young ladies lives they've ruint, and how they've gone worldwide, even though it's their first album. These same brothas is on the down-low, if Oprah's right, so they confused and stupid on top of being talentless. Like this one young blood that keeps texting Reo about getting down out back the Dollar General in Arlington. It's a wrong number, but that young moron won't give it up."

Leon smiled in silent amusement at the old codger getting riled up. Harding didn't pay him no mind and kept going. "It's like ol' Amos said in the Good Book: 'Thus saith the Lord: thy wife shall be a harlot in the city, and thy sons and thy daughters shall fall by the sword, and thy line shall be divided by a line; thou shalt die in a polluted land, and Israel shall surely go into captivity forth of his land.' That's where we is, Bumpi. But you know something, Bumpi? The good Lord still speaks to us. He led us out of Egypt, and he's going to lead this city out of this place of darkness. The righteous have heard, and we will cast off the shackles of the tyrant and make this land clean once again."

Leon exhaled and finished the old man's thought. "What Harding and me are trying to say is that we like what you're doing, and we're here to help. It's time we did some house cleaning, and we ain't going to leave it to you to do all of it."

A slender young man in baggy jeans and a clean wife-beater undershirt pulled up a chair next to old Harding. He had a thin mustache on his top lip, and his eyes sparkled with an intelligent mischief. Not the kind that ever took milk-money from defenseless kids smaller than him, but the kind that got even with those who did.

He entered the conversation in jest, saying, "So this is the black avenger? Hey man, I'm Reo. Where you from?"

Bumpi answered, "I am from the Congo. It is in Africa. It is a terrible place."

"So you really are an African-American?" Reo smiled.

"Yes. I am. But I want to just be an American. Africa is a bad place. Food is hard to come by. When you get it to eat, you have to watch it, or people steal it. There are soldiers everywhere, and they explode your hut and shoot your chicken for fun."

Reo smirked, "Man, that sounds like Frazier. How'd you get here? Did you punk dudes there, too?"

Bumpi shook his head "no". "The State Department of the United States gave me a visa and told me I would live here. In Congo, my family always run from bad guys, because they are so many and are not afraid to kill. Here there are not so many, and they are cowards. They are afraid if you fight back."

"Yeah. Where's your family at?"

"My father is dead. My mother is in Congo. I want to get a job for money to bring her here," Bumpi said, the homesickness in his heart evident. This was hard, being in this crime city without her. He had several houses that were burned to the ground as he fled, but home was always in her arms. He cried when he left his mother at the airport.

Leon said, "That's a hell of a story behind you. That'd make a heck of a blues song. You ever heard the blues before?"

"No. What is blues?"

Leon exhaled a plume of smoke as he looked over to the old man. "Harding, school your boy here." Leon stood up and walked to the far side of the diner. He picked up a worn acoustic guitar and carried it back to old Apricot's waiting hands. The old man took it, and Leon sidled up to the bar, ordering the young man named 4-way to pour him a whiskey.

Harding started strumming the guitar. "Now all you young bucks listen up. The blues is the source of all that is good in music. King David knew the blues. We used to sing it out in the fields, when we had chains. When we lost 'em, we put it to guitar. See, blues is the heart and soul of the black people: blues is about having it hard and ain't nothing you can do about it. Your heart want to love, but all it gets is hurt. Then all you can do is holler out that the Lord forgives you for all the bad you done did."

As Harding's strumming turned into soulful chords, he opened on up. "Young blood, the blues is everywhere. The Mississippi Delta is just the home of it getting set to music, but peoples everywhere feel the hurt. I miss my momma, too. I feel sorry for so many of the youngins, 'cause they ain't had no daddy like I did to even miss. But I got my lil' girl and her boy Reo."

"So you got nobody here?" asked Reo.

Bumpi answered, "No. I am alone."

"Until now," smiled Reo. "Why don't you come meet my mom? She'd love to make you dinner."

Bumpi smiled. "That is good. Yes, I would like that." He looked around the derelict diner before asking, "What do you all do here?"

The wiry, short young man behind the lunch counter piped up, "We run this bitch! We all up in this hood!" He then beat his chest through his sweaty undershirt and flashed some gang sign. It did not make him look impressive at all.

"It's more than that," came the soft voice of a giant young man in a red sweater, walking in through the back door and carrying some styrofoam take-out boxes. He looked at Bumpi and waved. "Hi, I'm Jerome. We keep trouble-makers out of our neighborhood. There's gangs all over the city running neighborhoods, so we made our own to keep the bad guys out. We had a falling out recently, but we worked it out."

Bumpi knew he was in the right place.

Jerome confirmed this when he asked, "You want some bar-b-que?"

Duke Willie was about to cast a plague on Memphis, if that Latina bitch and this damn African kept making things hard for him. After he had his secretary untie Devon and get his naked, black ass off his desk, Willie dug out of Devon enough

131

information to know who had fucked up his ends: that caramel-skinned, straight-haired mutha fucka Leon Johnson. Willie and him had crossed paths back in the day, when that Super Fly-looking dick stole Willie's girl. Willie had only beat the bitch when she had it coming, and this smooth-talking skillet rolled up and made off with her.

It was all put on lockdown and settled, though: after Duke Willie came to power, he had some friends condemn Leon's house and run over his momma outside church one Sunday. Leon learnt his place. He broke that trick, and to make sure the lesson stuck, Willie's boys would go smash a window or cut a tire now and then as a reminder. Yeah, Willie had a lot of people to do that to, but this one was personal. Just like the rest of 'em.

But now that mutha fucka was back. "Aight, Devon, this is how we gonna do it. Call out da ridaz."

"Sure thang, boss."

"Get them in touch wif me. They're gonna pay a little visit to Leon's hideout. Make sure they got the 7.62s, because these mutha fuckas are gonna spray that run-down chicken shack until they out of lead."

"Sure thang, boss."

"Then they gonna burn that mutha fucka down."

Devon nodded, the sweat beading down his chin onto his naked, hairy gut. There was going to come a plague on south Memphis tonight. Duke Willie's ridaz were going to take South Third straight to Hell.

Harding had just finished a medley of songs, when a rapid knock came at the front door to the Teahouse. 4-way jumped to, squaring off against the noise. Everybody got quiet, but Reo rose from his chair to look through the peep-hole. After he saw what stood outside, he motioned for everybody to relax.

Opening the door, the eyes of all inside fell on the scraggly crack-head standing in the pale, white street light. "Hey, dude. You need something?" asked Reo.

"How's you?" asked the frizzy-haired crack-head. "I got dis right here, and I'd like to sell you gentlemen dis fine garment," the hobo said, as he unrolled a pair of little girl-sized, pink sweat pants.

Reo motioned in the negative. "No, no we don't need none of that. If you need something to eat, take this," he finished, pulling a wrinkled $5 bill from his jeans pocket.

"Okay, thanks," said the hobo, as he quickly snatched the money and turned away.

Reo closed the door. He liked helping people, but he knew those sweat pants weren't that crack-head's, and he didn't want to encourage stealing.

A mere second after the door shut, Reo heard the hobo yell out, "Dey're in der!" and a torrent of gunfire opened up.

Bumpi hit the floor as the bullets and shattered glass rained like hail around him, the furious kind of rain that comes at you from the side, leaving you no chance for shelter.

He heard shouting from Leon for everybody to get down and the thuds of his saviors' bodies hitting the ground. He peaked his white eyes underneath his crooked elbow to try to see if anybody had been hit, but all he could see were some bodies on the ground. If they were bleeding their red blood, they were keeping it a secret for now.

The profusion of bullets, probably from an AK-47 (Bumpi could tell by the merciless way they tore through the walls), stormed into the Teahouse for what seemed like hours, when your mind clutches after every second, trying to see if this would be the last.

Then it stopped haltingly, like the last kernels of corn exploding in relentless heat. Bumpi knew there were only a few seconds the cloud of gun smoke would buy them before the enemy could see, so he sprung on all fours from the floor. He found Leon face down with his hands over the back of his head, who got right up when Bumpi pulled on the collar of his jacket. 4-way came scrambling out of the closet, stopping when the door became held fast by an unmoving Jerome. He held his massive stomach, blood oozing out between his fingers. It was a scratch, but when you get scratched the right way, it hurts like Hell on fire.

Harding came crawling out from behind the soda counter, but stopped all of a sudden. Bumpi stopped in his tracks when he saw the old man's eyes go wide with horror. Following Harding's eyes, he saw the limp, bullet-addled body of Reo lying on the counter. It looked like he had tried to jump to safety, but went up when he should have got down.

Without saying a word, Bumpi and Leon moved over calmly to pick up the body. Harding quietly stood up on his own. With Jerome leaning on 4-way, Harding kicked aside some of the pieces of the place that used to be like a home, clearing the way to the back door.

The old man didn't pay no mind to the debris littering his sweater, as he led the way out back. The others following after him, Harding crossed the broken parking lot, the night still hanging dark on the air. Bumpi and Leon and Jerome and 4-way caught up with Harding at the concrete drainage ditch behind the teahouse.

Without a look for steadying himself or a helping hand, Harding jumped the four feet down, his arthritis be damned. He embraced the pain of the landing, so he could quietly call up, "Throw Reo down to me."

Leon and Bumpi, silent and their white garments stained with blood, tenderly pass the young man into the shadows of the concrete ditch. The flickering light of the cold, yellow lamp

134

behind the building didn't show their way, but the white in Harding's beard gave them a star to aim by. The old man carried this burden.

The pair lept down, turning back only to help 4-way's diminutive frame get Jerome down to safety. When Jerome stepped down into the ditch, it took all free men to catch him, weak as he was with pain and bleeding. As they held him aright, Bumpi looked back to see the teahouse go up in flames.

Everybody carried somebody, as they filed down the defilade. After walking many moments in silence, Bumpi caught Reo's body as it slid off Harding's stooped, burly shoulders. He saw the blood from the old man's nephew had mixed with the tears leaking down Harding's face, quietly choking down the sorrow threatening him in his old age.

"Not long now," Leon said to Jerome, to keep his mind in the here and now. "You're gonna be okay."

"Don't take me to the Med. Willie can get me there," the husky man implored.

"No, we're gonna patch you up. I got a good doctor that makes house calls."

"He ain't got a dot on his forehead, does he? He speaks English?"

Leon chuckled. "No, blood, he's got one of them Jewish beanies on his head. See, Bumpi: I told you, you have fans all over town."

Bumpi did not expect this, for the Jews to be helping the blacks in Memphis. The Muslim missionary he met in the Congo said that Jews were evil and wanted to harvest orphans' organs to sell on the black market, and the Nation of Islam guy said pretty much the same thing. He would later come to find out that in this city, when whites and blacks didn't mix, the Jews often held out their hand to the blacks. There was a humility taught in the temples learned from years on the outside, that took several decades to reach the pulpits.

The men trudged along for a while longer in the dark, the shards of light from the street and porch lights only breaking through the fences and overgrowth in rare places.

Leon broke the silence, saying, "We're gonna head off this way, Harding," nodding his head to the side of the ditch. "We got a son of Israel to wake up."

Harding stopped shuffling and looked to Leon. He fumbled over his words, his bottom lip quivering. Leon waited patiently for him to ask, "Well, whatch you want me to do with Reo?"

Everybody looked to Leon. Bumpi was used to seeing his dead friends dragged away to be violated by their killers. He learned that in America, there was always enough of the dead left to bury.

Leon solemnly spoke, "Take him to his momma. Ain't nothin' doing for him now. Miss Gracey will hurt, but you gonna be strong for her. Right, Apricot?" He leveled his tired, resolute eyes to look into the red eyes in that old skull.

Harding worked his lips together, as if he was chewing on his tongue, but he nodded, looking away from Leon as soon as he understood he had to do what he was told. Bumpi started moving down the ditch, his back and shoulder aching a hot pain from carrying the young man's body. He was covered in blood, but when had that got in his way before?

Leon and 4-way helped Jerome scale the wall to escape the ditch and disappeared into the lush, green bushes growing unchecked along its banks.

Bumpi and Harding kept walking in the ditch, under cover of night. The ditch grew wet with the morning dew, and a chill kissed his bare skin. The blood covering him wasn't warm

136

anymore, but he could still feel it apart from the moist air cloying about him.

He slipped on a slick moss, falling forward, skinning his face on the concrete. Ol' Apricot tried to reach out for Reo's body to stop it from touching the ground, this unhallowed ground, but was too slow. His momentum carried him to the jumble of young men, one living, one dead, and he too fell to the ground, landing atop Reo.

His nephew's eyes had come open, the bloody tears framing his white eyes. Apricot could see his own breath come out on the young man. He could be strong no longer. He buried his face into the shattered breast of his blood, his kin.

Bumpi sat up, exhausted. He watched the old man mourn the young man in the morning dew.

When the African and the old man delivered her son to Miss Gracey, the drowsy woman stared at the body lying on the white wooden slats of her back porch. She pulled her hair net off and rubbed the sleep from her left eye, as though it hadn't noticed what the right had already seen. She reached down and touched the young man's face, as though these men had brought her an illusion, not her only son.

The two men stood there mournfully, bearing witness to the woman as she sank to her knees, her plain nightgown pulling back to expose her knees to the splintering wood. They stood there helpless, as she cried and wailed, clutching her dead son to the breasts that suckled the sweet young baby he had been.

As her sorrow became hysteria, they could offer her nothing to quiet her pain. A few sleepy and high neighbors came to investigate the wails they heard through the decrepit fence that Reo had just yesterday gotten the pieces to mend. He had gotten things set to right and was about to put it all back together.

That afternoon when Bumpi came to, he found himself unable to move. It wasn't because anybody had tied him up, but it did have something to do with the epic beat-down that Devon and Willie's goons had just paid to his account last night. Every breath felt like he was sucking fire; when he rolled from his side, his joints felt brittle, as though they were about to break apart. His entire body felt sore, like he was one big bruise holding together a bag of fractured bones. He hadn't felt this bad since the UN peacekeepers had played hide and seek with him and their Jeep.

He knew he wasn't going to die on this firm, doilie-addled daybed, but part of him wished he could. He felt some grief for the nice woman and the friends of the dead young man. But for Bumpi, he had seen far too much death. He had seen it too many times up close. He had heard it whistle to him like a piper enticing him to a home he didn't want to go to. Knowing he should feel bad for them was the best he could do emotionally; casting their Satan down from his throne was the only thing he could do to make Reo's sacrifice worth it.

But for now the searing ache inside him was his only companion. Until he heard a light tap on the door. "Come in," he said in his clean, blunt accent.

The chunky, glass doorknob clunked open, and in stepped one of the rarest sights Bumpi would ever see: a white man in South Memphis. This one was slightly tanned, from the sun, not a bottle. He had short, spiked, dark hair and wore a black, gold pin-striped suit. He reached his free hand out to Bumpi with the swagger of a good car salesman welcoming Bumpi to his lot.

He sat down and whipped off his gold aviators, as he firmly pressed his soft, strong hand with Bumpi's hard, bony fingers. "I'm truly sorry, for what happened. Reo was a good guy: he was really smart, had a lot of potential. He believed in the cause."

Bumpi ignored the pain and sat up indignantly at the assertion that there was a cause worth that mother's tears. "What do you mean, 'He believed in the cause'? You think he was a soldier for you in this place?"

"Yes, that's exactly what I mean. Not really for me, but…"

"Who are you, white man, that thinks he can have black men fight and die for you? What kind of piece of shit cause did you have him die for? What gang do you run that uses our lives for your own gain?!" Bumpi finished, his anger on clear display.

"Sir, you misunderstand me. He died for you," the white man said, his voice soft.

Bumpi didn't take his meaning.

"Reo and his boys wanted better for Memphis. Me and my boys wanted better for Memphis, and so did others. But to be honest, we grew so used to the shithole we're in, we forgot that we could shovel it out. Duke Willie hasn't been challenged since his fourth year in office, sixteen years ago. We just assumed he'd always be there, fucking up everything for everybody until the stars burned out, like some asshole pharaoh. But you showed us wrong."

The incredibly ebon man listened.

"Bumpi, this isn't my war, this is OUR war. You started this fight because you were sick of living like this. My people, Reo's people, other people in this city, you woke us up. You reminded us that we could do more if we'd quit our bitching and do the right thing."

Bumpi was awed: he knew he was doing something important, but he hadn't really thought through the vigilante crusade he launched. He was just sick of living under constant threat of violent murder at the hands of those in charge; it had never occurred to him that things might change. He figured he'd piss off the right people and wind up dead, but then he wouldn't have to deal with it anymore. He had never counted on anybody else caring. His burning ribs heaved, as he started to tear up against his will.

The white man leaned in, whispering, "We're gonna get you out of here. You're gonna get better, and then we're going to finish this. Together."

Duke Willie kicked his fuzzy, white slippers up onto the glass tabletop, smoldering cigar in his mouth, watching those white women wrestle in his pool. The night air helped steady his mind, through the cocaine rush and the marijuana mellow. He swapped the cigar for a snifter of Courvoisier and a smile, as he watched those fucking whores tear their tops off. He looked around his backyard recreation area, with the basketball court where his boys were playing, his swimming pool and hot tub full of hot, young bitches, and all the verdant greenery and faux-marble statues around the garden framing it all.

Life had gotten complicated with all his money-makers getting turned over to actual cops and that fucking African closing in on him. Things had gotten hot in town, and with all the evidence that was getting collected on him, Willie had announced he was considering retirement. That was before he heard how his ridaz had taken care of bidness, though. Life was all good now.

The sound of pistol clips sliding into place and revolver rounds being flipped into chamber clicked under the cover of darkness. A dozen people had this quiet, hidden cove on lock-down.

Princess checked his silver-plated revolver one last time. "You ready for the final act?" he asked the tall African who made all this possible.

Bumpi stacked his nickel-plated Desert Eagle and stared at the instrument of death. "It is time for we all to play our parts." He looked Princess in the eyes. "Tomorrow is a new day, or the Hell of today stretches on forever."

Princess inspected the group assembled, including Spectre, Bumpi, ol' Harding, Leon, a healed Jerome, 4-way, and members of every angry constituency in Memphis that wanted to see Duke Willie brought down with extreme prejudice. "Looks good," he muttered. "Everybody remember their parts?"

"I'm gonna climb into this here death-trap," said Harding, pointing to a modified, industrial-use dump truck. "And I'm going to smash through the front gate. And the rest of the house, if all y'all get pumped full of lead."

"Good enough," agreed Spectre. "I'm going to take you ne'er-do-wells and clear the outlying buildings," he says, gesturing to almost half the group.

"Jerome, you two, and I will enter and clear the main house," reminded Princess. "4-way, uh, stay here and keep watch."

"Whu?! I'm gonna pop a cap in some ass, yo," countered 4-way, as he rocked his .38 loaded with blanks (Jerome had loaded it for him) like somebody who'd never actually hit a target before.

"Exactly, and I'm afraid that ass will be one of ours. I've seen you shoot," said Leon. "You and Harding are to watch the entrance and keep an eye out for any funny business."

4-way popped his bony chin high into the air, which measured almost five feet, six inches from the ground. That would do, it seemed.

Bumpi stopped and reflected: he was about to help bring down a dictator. Things might actually get better here in his new home, like they never would in the Congo.

Leon prayed silently. Justice was about to be done, not just for him, but for everyone.

Princess and Spectre had already come to terms with what trials and tribulations lay ahead in this crusade they were about to launch. It started now.

Harding would be able to tell his grandson Reo that they finally got that dirty bastard, next time he visited his grave. Harding knew Reo was in Heaven watching. He would see his people freed from pharaoh.

Duke Willie mused to himself how he probably had another twelve years in power if his luck held, and he could die of a stroke while making it rain on some bitches. That bootlick newspaper would never reveal all the details of his dirty business, assuming the Memphis PD even gave it to them. He laughed as he thought about the looks on the faces of the sad sack city reporter and his editor if the police showed it to them, just to fuck with them. "Oh, that would be sweet," he started to say.

A loud splash interrupted his reverie. Duke Willie looked down at the pool, expecting to see some giggling nymphs making with the splashy-splashy. What he saw was Devon's fat ass in his suit floating in the water. "No, that's not sexy at all," he thought.

It took a minute for his drug-addled perceptions to register the screaming of the girls as they ran away from the pool, but when it did, he got really alarmed. Alarmed enough for a stoned man to stand up; I don't know if you've ever been stoned, but that is a big deal.

Looking around his back yard, he didn't see any of his bitches anywhere. The basketball was on the court, and that was the only thing the spotlight showed. He staggered in his terry-cloth robe, looking for any sign of normalcy. "Where'd everybody go?" he muttered to nobody else.

As his gaze wandered, he caught a glimpse of something as high and dark as a black sun between him and his swimming pool. "Ah," he panted in fear, staggering back on his flip flops.

"Do not move, Duke Willie. Yes, I am talking to you," ordered Bumpi, standing there in a black track suit.

"Oh, shit," Willie said breathlessly, raising his hands in a pantomime of self-defense. Once upon a time, those hands were powerful and could drop even strong men with a single blow. Now they were so rotten with sin and age that they were only useful for clubbing the defenseless. "I thought you wuz dead."

Bumpi cocked the nickel-plated Desert Eagle in his left hand. Willie's eyes focused at the sound.

"Now that I have your attention, it is good for you to know that you are surrounded. All of your 'real peoples' cannot help you now," he continued in his halting, powerful English.

Duke Willie nodded his gray head in understanding. "Okay, if that's how it's got to go down, I got you…"

Bumpi was secretly relieved to hear the resignation in Duke Willie's voice. He and the rest of the crew had taken down Willie's men and servants without firing a shot, no casualties on either side. Maybe the bloodshed had already stopped.

"MOTHA FUCKA!!!" screamed Duke Willie, as he pulled a 9mm pistol out of his slightly damp, white terry-cloth robe and started shooting. He didn't give a damn how that

African bastard got past his security: Willie was a fighter, and he would handle this bullshit his own self!

Bumpi dropped expertly down to the ground immediately, having an unfortunate amount of experience in dodging bullets. He cursed himself for walking out into the open with no cover, but damn it, how many people carry around guns in their bath robes?!

But Bumpi had cover, of the kind that shoots at the guy shooting at you. Leon stepped out from behind the brick wall at the edge of the house to fire a controlled pair of shots, hoping to suppress or scare into submission Duke Willie. Leon was burning for revenge, but he and all the rest had to remember: Duke Willie was still the mayor of the city. It wouldn't do to leave a man like that in a pool of lead and blood, when they were trying to make this a better place. They had to take him alive.

One shot tore through the sleeve of Willie's left arm, but bit no flesh. Willie turned and fired at Leon's head and would have put some nasty perforations in it, had Leon not ducked back into the shadows.

Bumpi scrambled to take Willie's legs out from under him, but he was too slow: Duke Willie frog-stomped him with both feet into the travertine marble. Bumpi collapsed onto the ground, the wind crushed out of his lungs. Duke Willie raised a flip-flop up to bring down on the African avenger's head, but before he could, Spectre appeared out of the darkness with a flying drop-kick, knocking Willie off his prey.

Duke Willie fell to the ground, and Spectre landed with a loud thud. "AH! My back's not as young as it used to be. Oh," the nigh-60 year old man in black exclaimed.

Princess rushed through the glass doors leading from the living room out to the pool, bringing a shiny, black dress shoe up into Willie's massive face. The mayor flopped back down to the ground, but when Princess reared back for another stroke, Willie grabbed the shiny, freshly polished shoe still on the ground and pulled, sending the dark-haired assailant to join a gasping Bumpi on the travertine.

Duke Willie barely had time to wipe the blood from his eyebrow, staining his clean white robe crimson, when the guardians at the gate, old Harding and 4-way, came screaming out of the house at him.

Reclaiming his ground, Duke Willie dealt with them, one fist at a time. One ham-sized fist planted a well-aimed shot so pretty to make even the most paid-off boxing judge swoon firmly into the squished face of 4-way, knocking him out cold. His right hand grabbed Harding by the sweater vest and pulled him forward, throwing the old man off balance. With 4-way down, Willie turned to the senior citizen and pushed him into the pool.

By this time, Bumpi's breath had returned enough for him to begin to rise. Problem was, Duke Willie was already up and within ass-kicking distance. Willie put his considerable weight behind the fist he brought across Bumpi's face, dazing but not sending him down. No, Duke Willie grabbed Bumpi up by his collar and flung him into the roiling waters to join a splashing and kicking Harding.

Willie bent down to pick up the Desert Eagle that had just been in his face. It was time for these punk bitches to get what was coming to them, he decided. Taking it in hand, he aimed it first at that damn African, then he would take the old man; those little fuckers Princess and Spectre were next; and then that punk Leon was going to get his score settled.

Or that was his plan, at least, until he heard gunshots going off all around him. He didn't take the time to look for the myriad directions they were coming from, he just took off running for the grill pit. Willie remembered that the grill was

145

surrounded by brick walls that had a better chance of stopping a bullet than terry-cloth.

As the rounds blasted all around him, causing a secondary chorus of busting glass and breaking bricks, Duke Willie ran, every second in his adrenaline and drug-addled mind soaking in the thrill of the fight. IT WAS ON!

Duke Willie leapt across the grill pit wall, shockingly agile for a 60+ year-old man. He rolled in the air, landing on his back. His face was overtaken by an excited leer.

And immediately crest-fallen when a shiny .38 revolver started pointing right between his eyes. Leon smiled at him, half of his caramel and black visage illuminated by the light of the court beside him.

Willie looked at him, still, except for his heavy breathing.

Man, Leon wanted to pull that trigger. His momma, his woman, his life had been wrecked by this man. Sure, he and the gang had agreed to a plan on what to do with Willie, but plans can get screwed up and not go the way you wanted to. Now a bullet, well, that just goes the way you point it. It's simple that way: there wouldn't be no squabbling or figuring out what to do with Willie, or the threat he might make a come-back. Simplicity was just a click away.

But Leon was a man of his word, a man of honor. His momma wouldn't want her boy to become a killer; Jesus never told him to kill nobody. Leon motioned for Willie to get up and back over to the pool.

Putting down the Desert Eagle, Willie got up, raising his hands to show he was defenseless. Leon walked him over to the rest of the crew, who had gotten off their backs and out of the pool. Regardless of how they got there, they were all angry.

Princess snatched up the Desert Eagle, handing it back to Bumpi, the man who made all this possible. Arraying themselves in a firing line, every gun was cocked and aimed.

146

Willie stopped where Leon directed him, kneeling down where he stopped. Not looking up, Duke Willie said, "I'm ready. Go ahead and do it."

"Do what?" Bumpi said.

Now Willie was the one getting impatient. He looked up at the African to tell him, "Listen, are you going to put a bullet in my head, or what? That's what you came for right? To kill me?"

Bumpi's face showed his desire for revenge for the blood that was spilled, but it was replaced by restraint. There was some Old Testament justice that he had the chance to lay down right now. "No. You are the mayor. This is a place where votes make the laws. So no, I will not kill you, though you deserve it. You have all the blood on your hands to make it right."

Exasperated, Duke Willie asked, "So why did y'all cock your shit and aim it at me?"

"To get your attention," said Spectre.

Willie was partly relieved, offering, "Then what the fuck are we doing here? I got some blow, let's draw a line and talk this out!"

"No drugs," answered Bumpi. "You will resign tonight. You will no more be mayor of this city. You will go away and hurt these people no more."

Before Willie could respond, strolling out into the backyard came AJ Plimpton, a dapper, older black gentleman with a pep in his step. He started talking before he saw the shit that was going down, saying, "Hey, Willie, the door was open, so I just let myself...Oh, Heeell no!"

Willie saw a desperate opportunity and tried to take it. "AJ! Come over here! I want you guys to meet my campaign manager, AJ! Come on, AJ!"

Without missing a beat, AJ rocked back on his heels and snapped his fingers, pointing at the erstwhile mayor. "I'm

147

good. Y'all have a nice night!" he said, as he turned on his heels and sauntered out.

Willie spat out, "Aw, shit."

Bumpi ordered, "Willie, you will step down. Now and for good. Never trouble Memphis again."

He was stuck. Willie started to nod his head in acceptance.

Suddenly, Princess barked at him, "And then you're going to stand for re-election, and fuck it all up!"

The group went quiet, unsure of what to say. The look of stunned bewilderment on Willie's face summed up the feelings of the group. "Why would I do that?"

Princess energetically stammered out his explanation. "Because then your backers will know you're a crazy fuck-up they can't trust anymore. You'll burn all your political capital and any goodwill you had left in the city. No one will trust you to clean toilets when it's all done."

Even though Willie was on his knees with half a dozen guns pointed at him, he didn't even try to disguise his disgust. "That's stupid," he said.

Leon joined in, saying, "Yeah, he should just step down. The rest of that kinda seems unnecessary." The rest of the group nodded their heads, except for Spectre. He just smiled.

Princess persevered. "Shut up! I'm really high right now, and I'm the one with the Masters in Political Science! So just shut up and go with it!"

As the talkers in the group started arguing over what Duke Willie was to do to ensure that he would never be a pox on the people of Memphis again, Bumpi uncocked his gun and relaxed. While Duke Willie stood on his knees and intense confusion overtook him, Bumpi was glad this drama was over. In a very real way, he had given back to the country that gave him this chance at a better life.

The Authors of Memphis Dirty

Stephen Clements is the publisher at LCG, author of Canopy of Heaven, editor of Call Me Tennessee, short story writer featured in many publications, and RPG editor to the greats. In his free time, he likes to drink and play with puppies.

Jeff Klitzner wrote the epic autobiography Call Me Tennessee, but he won't be writing a sequel. He really liked cheap beer and weed. The River Hippies Like Me is a side story to Call Me Tennessee.

JT Davenport is an idea man, master of the Void, and student of the blade. His life stories are all like Night Journey, and all without drugs! He's naturally like this!

Joseph Tate is friend of all children and can be seen flying around Tokyo, fighting space monsters with his sharp claws and fiery breath.